WITH AN UNOPENED UMBF

# WITH AN UNOPENED UMBRELLA IN THE POURING RAIN

Short stories by Ludovic Bruckstein

Translated from the Romanian by Alistair Ian Blyth

# Contents

# With an Unopened Umbrella in the Pouring Rain

Iapa is a village in Maramureş a few kilometres from Sighet with a few hundred chimneyed houses that stretch from down below, from the place called Boundary Valley, or Ciarda, or Chebliţe, from the bank of the River Tisza, which here flows broad and slow, making it a good place for barges to moor. Then the houses stretch along the edge of a road that climbs the hills to the places named Grui and Sihei and Meia, before scattering along the edge of the fir and oak forests.

It may well be precisely the village's position that made its inhabitants' occupations so various. There were ploughmen and carters, shepherds and traders, woodcutters and day labourers, and all kinds of other occupations arising from the village's proximity to the town, to the River Tisza, and also to the forest.

On Friday evening, for example, the Jewish bargemen's rafts used to moor here on their way downstream from logging in Poienile de sub Munte, Ruscova, Petrova, and Leordina; with thick hawsers they tethered their rafts to knotty willow stumps at the water's edge and went to spend the Sabbath with a family whose house served as a makeshift inn, where they found lodging that was cheap and sometimes even free of charge. On Friday evening and Saturday morning, they joined the congregation in the tradesmen's synagogue, softly murmuring their prayers, and as evening fell, they seated themselves at the end of a long table in the same synagogue, munching dried herring tails with a crust of *koyletch*. Often, they cracked walnuts, sipped strong slivovitz, and hummed old, wordless songs at that *shaloshudes* meal, the third of the Sabbath, provided by one of the synagogue's trustees. And in the evening, after a hurried *maariv* and *havdalah* prayer and the song of parting from Queen Sabbath, recited when they could see at least three stars clearly in the deep blue sky, the Jewish bargemen returned to the riverbank and shook hands with the Romanian bargemen. For they too had come down from Leordina, Petrova, and Poienile de sub Munte to moor their rafts, tethering them to the same knotty willow stumps before going to spend their Sunday in the village. After which they unmoored their rafts and went on their way, down the Tisza …

In the place named Ciarda, or Cheblițe, in the valley between the river Tisza and the hill, all along the main road, there lived a hundred and twenty Jewish families, who earned their bread, which was not always daily bread, from many different occupations: there were numerous woodcutters, one carter, and five porters, who early each morning hung a thick sack across their chests and one over their backs and set off to the loading ramp of Sighet station, where they filled them with flour or firewood or whatever need to be loaded and unloaded from the freight cars; there were seekers of work or simply seekers of bread, vagrants who set out on Sunday with an empty bag and returned on Friday having filled it with dry crusts and a greater or lesser quantity of those small grey coins with a hole in the middle; there were also five or six cattle traders, who sweated and grew hoarse on market days; and then there were four grocers, three butchers, two cobblers, two poor tailors, two carpenters, and a blacksmith.

Well, it is of that blacksmith that I wish to tell you a tale: Schmiel the Blacksmith, as he was called, since nobody in the village could remember his surname. And I also wish to tell you the tale of Rifka, his wife, and of their children, whose number nobody knew for sure, since they came into the world and grew up like the grass, like the weeds, like the flowers…

The house of Schmiel the Blacksmith was at the meeting of the ways, where the country road that led to Sighet met the path that led up into the forest. It was a small cottage, painted dark blue, with a porch and two rooms. Behind the house was a field with a shed for a cow, and behind the shed there was a vegetable patch. The smithy was an extension on one side of the house: two log walls adjoining the firewall, roofed with shingles, with an opening that rested on two slender poles of fir. Between these poles was a post for tethering the horses waiting their turn to be shod, which would wait patient and resigned, slowly chewing the hay their masters put before them. Beneath the shingle roof there was also a bench: an old, cracked plank on which the horses' owners sat, filling their pipes with cheap shag tobacco, slowly smoking and exchanging a word or two with the blacksmith. Inside, within the smithy, by the wall at the back, were the brick furnace, with its bellows of old patched leather, the anvil, which rested on a thick stump, hammers and tongs, iron hoops and bars in the corner – all of it black with soot.

Schmiel the Blacksmith was a short, well-built man with hair as black as pitch, cropped short beneath a greasy cap, with a tangled black beard that framed a toil-worn face. The skin of his face was like parchment, yellow, leathery, scored by deep wrinkles, covered in soot, so much so that it looked as if it had been drawn in ink by a master's hand. The soot never left those wrinkles, even though every Friday afternoon Schmiel went to the *mikve*, the communal bath, where first he entered the sauna, climbing to the highest bench and mercilessly lashing himself with the whisk, after which he went to the pool, where he thrice immersed himself before climbing back out, his soul clean, lighter, at peace. But before this ritual immersion, standing up to his chest in the warm, cloudy water of the *mikve*, he would exchange a few words with the other Jews from the village, asking about bread, children, health, the affairs of the community, the village, the country, the world. After this, he closed his eyes and mouth, pinched his nose between finger and thumb, and submerged himself thrice in succession. Having returned home, he would put on his best clothes in order to greet the Sabbath in the proper way. And until the evening of the next day the smithy, horses, horseshoes, hammer, anvil no longer existed; nothing else existed.

On Friday evening and Saturday morning, he went to the trades-men's synagogue and murmured prayers that he intuited sooner than understood. At home, after the meal, he would doze in his chair and sing snatches of hymns he had heard but not understood, for he had not studied very long at the *heyder*, since from a very early age he had been closely acquainted with toil for a living. And this was one of his secret sorrows: he could spell out the letters of the words in books, but he didn't understand them.

The folk in the village knew his habits. If a horseshoe happened to fall off on the Sabbath, the peasant would take the horse to the smithy without calling to Schmiel to come out of the house, he would tether it to the post beneath the roof of the lean-to smithy, place a sack of hay before it and, going about his business, leave it there to wait on its own. And the horse would wait patiently, slowly chewing the hay; it would wait until the three stars appeared in the deep blue sky. And the horse's owner would look up at the sky and count the stars, to know when he could go to fetch his freshly shod horse.

For, on Saturday evening, after he counted at least three stars in the sky, Schmiel would pour slivovitz in a little glass, to the brim, ready to pour it over the corner of the table, that the week, the coming week, might be full. Rifka, his wife, would light two candles, which she gave to one of the smaller of their sons, to hold them up as high as he could, that the week, the coming week, might be luminous. And Schmiel would take the little glass in his sinewy hand and solemnly recite the prayer of parting from the Sabbath, and then he would drink half the strong slivovitz and pour the rest of the glass over the corner of the table; he would take the two candles from the boy's hand and extinguish them by dipping them in the slivovitz on the table, and the liquor would catch fire, burning with a translucent blue flame, lighting up the happy faces of those standing around: Schmiel, Rifka, their seven children, or eight, or nine, who knows now how many. And Schmiel would sing 'Hamavdil,' the old hymn of bidding the Sabbath farewell, whose words he didn't really understand, but which he had heard sung exactly the same way by his father, who had heard them from his grandfather, who had herd them from his great-grandfather, and so on. And the whole family, Rifka and the sons and daughters, would hum along.

After the final strains of the hymn died away, the spell was broken and everything returned to normal. Schmiel quickly put on his work clothes, his leather apron, and would go to the smithy to shoe the horse of Gheorghe the Trusty's son, or the horse of Ion the Drummer's son – for he recognised the horse of every man in the village and neighbouring villages – while Rifka worked the bellows with her foot, rhythmically pumping her leg up and down. She was a small, thin, lively woman, and to lend more weight to the bellows, she would stamp as hard as she could, as if she were dancing a jig on the narrow wooden handle. And when she felt herself beginning to tire, she would press her hand on the knee of the leg pumping the bellows.

And Schmiel would grip the red-hot iron with the tongs, he would hammer it on the anvil, beating and shaping a beautiful horseshoe, the perfect, most comfortable fit for the horse …

And the sparks would dance and flash …

The smithy wasn't Schmiel's only trade, although it was his main occupation, from which he earned his daily bread. But when there wasn't work to do shoeing horses or fitting hoops to the wheel of some cart, Schmiel would mow hay on the hills around the village. He was a mower of renown, and when he spat in his palms and grasped the handles of the scythe, when he felled broad swaths of hay, few were those who could keep up with him.

Likewise, pumping the smithy bellows was far from being his wife Rifka's only occupation. Or even the most important one. On her small head, always tied with the same brown, sun-faded scarf, and on her thin, bony shoulders, she bore a host of cares, large and small. Keeping the house clean, washing the clothes, darning the socks, hoeing and weeding the garden, cooking the food for her husband and the seven or eight or however many children there were. And above all, taking care of the cow. The cow had to be groomed, fed, and milked twice a day. And every day the milk had to be taken to market in the town of Sighet.

Rifka woke up at the crack of dawn, before anybody else in the house, she lit the fire in the hearth, she set the pot of beans or pota-toes to boil on the iron hob, and then she shouldered the bag with the two jugs of milk and set off to Sighet. At around midday she would return from the town with the empty jugs and a few pennies tightly knotted in her handkerchief; she would dish out the food, which had boiled in the meantime, ladling it into the tin plates, and they would all eat heartily.

This is what she did every working day that the Lord gave her on this earth.

Once only did things happen differently and the tale of Rifka's misadventure was told in the village ever thereafter.

One morning, she was on the way to market in Sighet with the jugs of milk when all of a sudden, she came to a stop, affrighted. And she began to rack her brains. She had lit the fire in the hearth, that was for sure… She had placed the pot of water on the hob, that was for sure … But she couldn't remember whether or not she had tossed the beans in the water. Would she arrive back home at midday and find food to put on the table for her husband and children? She didn't know what to do or how to rescue the situation.

Downcast and anxious, she met Sura-Beile, a neighbour, who was on her way home after selling a few eggs in town.

'Sura-Beile, my dear, you'll never guess what's happened … please go to my house and throw a handful of beans in the pot!'

The neighbour promised to do as she said and so Rifka went on her way, reassured. But after a little while, she was overcome with uneasiness once more. 'Does Sura-Beile have nothing else to worry about except my pot?' she thought to herself, *By the time she gets home, she'll have forgotten. And if not, once she gets home, she'll be so busy with her children and her hens that she'll forget about my pot, in which there's nothing but water cooking…*

She then met Malke, the grocer's wife.

'Dear Malke, God placed you in my path, you'll never guess what's happened… As soon as you get home, go and throw a handful of beans in my pot!'

Malke promised her she would and Rifka went on her way, at peace. But not for very long. *That Malke, as soon as she gets home, I can see her now, she'll have to tend to the customers in her shop, one will be wanting a pound of salt, another a bottle of cooking oil, another a pair of laces… She'll forget all about my pot, in which water is boiling with nothing in it…*

Then she saw Haya, the daughter of Hersch-Leib the carter, on her way home in her two-horse cart.

'Haya, dear, if you hold God in your soul, go straight to my house and toss a handful of beans in the pot over the fire!'

Haya promised her she would, but Rifka had walked no more than a few paces before she felt uneasy once more. *That Haya is like a boy, Hersch-Leib doesn't have any sons, just four daughters, and that girl is the eldest, so she's like ten sons to him. She'll arrive home,* unharness the horses, give them their oats, bring them a bucket of water, curry them, and then she'll have to harness them again in a hurry, so that she can take the cart to the woods to fetch firewood… And that wretched pot will carry on boiling pointlessly, with nothing but water in it…

And so the smith's wife asked another two or three women from the village to throw beans in her pot after that.

At midday, Rifka arrived home all in a rush, with her empty jugs and a few pennies tightly tied in her handkerchief, and with fear in her soul.

On the hob the pot was bubbling away, full to overbrimming with beans. And that day her husband and children ate their fill as they never had before…

Trees grow slowly, but grass grows quickly. Weeds and flowers grow quickly, too. But it's as if nothing grows more quickly than a daughter. Barely do her parents have time to take a breath and look around than she has grown up, her body has filled out, and she's ready to be married off.

And so it was with the daughters of Schmiel the Blacksmith. Not one of them presented the slightest difficulty. They didn't have dowries, they didn't have trousseaus, they weren't choosy, and their parents weren't picky. Young men appeared over the horizon, they went out with the girls for a time, and then they got married, as naturally as could be, as naturally as the sun rising in the morning, as naturally as rain falling from a cloud or as the wind blowing.

The eldest daughter, Sara, married a young man by the name of Nahum Herschovitch, from the neighbouring village of Sarasău, who struggled to make a living at first, trying his hand at all kinds of trades, from porter to hawker of shoelaces, before learning to be a tinsmith in Sighet, after which he went to try his luck in a large town where he worked on galvanised tin roofs and roofs treated with red lead, and where he made gutters and drainpipes. The second eldest daughter, Reizel, married a boy from Borscha, the son of poor but hardworking folk. The young Reizel and Mendel Steinberg lived in the house of his parents, who had a bakery, or rather an old oven in their kitchen, where they baked fresh loaves every night, which they sold in the morning to the tavern keepers from the village and the neighbouring villages. On Friday evening, they put their neighbours' clay pots of bean dish, *csolent*, in the hot oven and took them out on Saturday afternoon, done to a turn. And that was how they earned a modest living, day by day…

It never crossed the mind of either Schmiel or Rifka to oppose any of their daughters' marriages; it never crossed their minds for even an instant to want any other son-in-law than the one allotted to them by the Lord Above.

This was why the amazement of the whole family and all the people in the village and the neighbouring villages was all greater when Schmiel opposed his third daughter's marriage. And he opposed it with a stubbornness of which nobody could have imagined him capable.

The young man was from Remeți, another village on the Tisza, the son of poor, upstanding farmers. True, the lad didn't profess any trade in particular, but nor had Schmiel's other sons-in-law when they married, although afterward they had managed to make a living for themselves. But that wasn't the sticking point. Haim, the son of Moishe-Yankel from Remeți, was, after all, a good, big-hearted, hard-working lad skilled at everything from doing the laundry and keeping the house clean, from tending the apple orchard to chopping firewood, in a word, a lad 'for both Kiddush and Havdalah,' as they say. And to top it all, he was handsome, tall and as strong as a pine tree.

But Schmiel the Blacksmith wouldn't hear of him. Not for the life of him. And the reason quickly revealed itself: for Hana he wanted a man of letters, a learned man, a *talmid-hohem*. If he didn't have any book learning, then let at least one of his sons-in-law be a learned man. And with which daughter had he hoped to achieve this if not with Hana?

In truth, Hana was the most beautiful of his daughters. Slim, dark-eyed, with arched eyebrows and thick black wavy hair. Not that you could say that her young suitor didn't know anything at all. Moshe-Yankel's son Chaim had studied at the *heyder* school in Remeţi for a short time, he had done a little 'humesh and Rashi' – Torah and commentaries – but truth be told, when it came to those huge tomes with the tiny letters in the margins, the *ghemarah* and *tosafot*, he didn't know a single thing.

The two youngsters were in love, and so they were devastated. They met in secret, at the bottom of the garden; wandered like lunatics in the middle of the day, pale-faced, wild-eyed. They lost their appetites for food, work, life. Something had to be done. And so in secret, the lad's parents took counsel with Rifka, the girl's mother, and with other relatives from the two villages, and they decided to take the case to Reb Motl, the *shadkhan* from Sighet, to let him try to persuade the stubborn Schmiel to do something, in the name of God, because otherwise nobody else would be able to do anything and it would end in tragedy…

Reb Motl-shadkhan was a mediator by profession and his fame was well deserved. He was small and hunchbacked, he had lost the sight of his left eye, and his beard was a flaming red, but his mouth worked like well-oiled clockwork and he had a piercing mind: you could never gainsay him because he always agreed with whatever you said, but even so, you always found yourself adopting whatever it was that he advised.

And so Reb Motl-shadkhan arrived one evening to talk to Schmiel the Blacksmith. They sat at the table, each drinking a tot of strong slivovitz.

'He's a good boy, well-behaved,' began the *shadkhan*.

'Yes.'

'He's hardworking, industrious.'

'Yes! Nobody is saying he isn't.'

'His family are decent folk.'

'Yes, there's no denying it.'

'Then what have you got against him?' blurted Reb Motl-shadkhan angrily.

'He's got no book learning!'

'No book learning? No book learning, you say? How do you know that, *reb* Schmiel, how do you know he has no book learning?' bristled *reb* Motl.

'All right, maybe he has a little, he knows his 'humesh and Rashi,' but he doesn't know anything from those big books! He doesn't know the *ghemarah*! He doesn't know the *toisefes*!'

'Vey, vey, vey,' said the *shadkhan*, shaking his head. 'A great sin to speak ill of somebody so blameless…'

'A sin? Blameless?' said Schmiel the Blacksmith, taking fright.

'That's right, because he's a modest lad, he doesn't show off, he doesn't boast… What, did you see it written on his nose that he doesn't have any book learning? What if I, Reb Motl-shadkhan, tell you that he knows how to study the *ghemarah* and the *toisefes*? And what if he comes here and reads you a page from the Talmud-Bavli, what will you say then?'

'Then… then… I'll see… we'll see…' stammered Schmiel evasively, and regarded him sceptically, as if he were a man who must be joking.

But Reb Motl stood up, as if he were personally offended, and said harshly, imperiously, 'Then know you, Reb Schmiel, that next week, on Thursday evening, I shall come here with Moshe-Yankl's son Chaim, and here in your house, here at this table, here in front of you, he will read to you a page from the Talmud.'

No sooner said than done. The *shadkhan* – not an empty-headed man, for he himself could decipher those big books with the tiny letters in the margins quite well – took the young Chaim home with him, chose a nice passage from the Talmud, from the Shabbat Tractate, and set about teaching him how to read and translate it: *Tanu Rabanan…* our elders taught us… *khadan et khavero lekaf zekhut, danim oto bizkhut*… he who judges his neighbour for the good will himself be judged for the good…

The young man visited the *shadkhan* a number of times, he had a good head, but he also strove very hard, he knew what he stood to lose and what he stood to gain. And so the next week, on the Thursday evening, Reb Motl-shadkhan arrived at the house of Schmiel Blacksmith with a large *ghemarah* tucked under his arm, followed by Moshe-Yankl's son Chaim from Remeți.

The light of the lamp hanging from the ceiling beam fell directly on the fresh white tablecloth laid by Rifka. Around the table *reb* Motl-shadkhan, the young Chaim, and Schmiel the Blacksmith took their places. Rikfa stood back, next to the seated children, silently waiting in the half-shadows near the freshly-whitewashed stove. And Hana sat hidden behind her mother, her eyes moist with emotion, voicelessly mouthing the prayer she had composed in her mind.

*Reb* Motl-shadkhan solemnly laid the huge *ghemarah* in front of the young man, who opened it, and Motl's face turned as white as chalk in fear… How could he have done such a thing? Instead of the Shabbat Tractate, he had brought a different tome, and not just any tome, but the Gitin Tractate, the one about divorce… An ill omen… All was now lost! For the first time in his life, Motl-shadkhan had blundered, and he alone was to blame. Such a blunder, such carelessness. He felt like banging his head against the wall, nothing less.

But the young man, after casting him a fugitive glance, lowered his eyes to the open book and in a clear, singsong voice, following the written lines with his eyes, he read:

'*Tanu Rabanan*… our elders teach us… *khadan et khavero lekaf zekhut*… he who judges his neighbour for the good… *danim oto lezekhut*… he too will be judged for the good…'

'What a good boy!' *reb* Motl said to himself with a sigh of relief. 'He learned the passage by heart, word for word!'

And in his mind the *shadkhan* decided, 'He deserves to be happy.'

The young man spoke on, in a grave, solemn voice, without lifting his eyes from the big book: '…*umaase be'ad chad*… and the story is told of a man, who came down from upper Galilee and entered the service of a man in the south for three years. On the eve of the Day of Atonement, he told his master: "Give me the wages I am owed and I will go to feed my wife and children." The master told him: "I have no money." The man said: "Give me fruit!" He said: "I have none." The worker said: "Give me land!" "I have none." "Give me cattle!" "I have none." "Then give me pillows and mattresses!" "I have none." The worker said nothing more. And he took his tools on his back… *vekhalakh lebeito, befakhei nefesh*… and he went home with a bitter soul, full of sadness…'

In the room there was deep silence. Schmiel the Blacksmith listened wide-eyed in amazement.

The young man continued:

'…*le-akhar kharegel*… after the holy day, the master took the man's wages and he also took three asses, one loaded with food, one loaded with drink, and one loaded with all manner of sweet fruits, and he brought them to the house of the worker. After they had eaten and drunk, he said to him: "When you told me, 'Give me my wages,' and I said, 'I have no money,' what did you suspect?" "I said to myself: 'Perhaps cheap goods were offered to you and you paid money for them…'" "And when you told me, 'Give me cattle!' and I told you, 'I have none,' what did you suspect?" "I said to myself, perhaps you have given them to others as a bond." "When you told me, 'Give me land!' and I told you, 'I have no land,' what did you suspect?" "I said to myself, 'Perhaps he has rented it to others.'" "And when I said to you, 'I have no fruit,' what did you suspect?" "I said to myself, 'Perhaps they are not yet tithed.'" "And when I told you, 'I have no pillows or mattresses,' how did you judge me?" "I said to myself, 'Maybe he has made an offering of all his wealth to Heaven…'" And then the master said to him, "*Khaavoda! Kakh khaya!* By all that is holy, so it was!

I made a covenant for all my wealth, because of my son, Khirkanos, who did not want to learn the Tora ... And when I went to my friends in Negev, on the eve of Yom Kippur, on the eve of the Day of Atonement, they absolved me of all my debts ... And you, just as you judged me for the good, so too will the Lord judge you for the good."'

Schmiel the Blacksmith sat motionless on his chair and looked at the young man. He looked at him with wide, moist eyes, and he listened to those wise words from the book of our ancestors. And he would have sat and listened longer, for days and nights in a row, he would have sat and listened, but the young man had finished.

Finally, wiping his eyes with the sleeve of his coat, Schmiel the Blacksmith said, 'Then, yes ... if he knows, then he knows ...'

That was all he said.

And before seven weeks had passed, the wedding was held.

And in this way, yet another marriage decided upon up in heaven and placed in the care of *reb* Motl-shadkhan was fulfilled down here, on earth.


Schmiel the Blacksmith was born in the village of Iapa, in that place known as Boundary Valley, or Csarda, or Chebilțe, and he lived his whole life in those places, between the Tisza Valley and the forests of the Gruiu and Siheiu hills. In his life he travelled only on foot or by cart, as far as the surrounding villages of Maramureș. The longest journey he took was as far as Borscha, where once he went by cart with other members of the congregation to hear the Shabbat-HaGadol sermon given by a famous itinerant rabbi, and he returned home full of goodness and repentance for sins he hadn't committed, and the largest town he ever saw was Sighet, with its handful of two-storey buildings in the centre of town and its two three-storey buildings.

But here he was, at the age of almost fifty, having to fret, to think about a long, long journey into the unknown ...

It so happened that after they wed, the young Hana, Schmiel's third and most beautiful daughter, and Chaim, the son of Moishe-Yankl from Remeți, lived *oif kest* in the house of Schmiel the Blacksmith for a few months, which is to say, 'on the food' of the bride's father, before staying for another few months in the house of the groom's father, in Remeți. After which they had to make their own way in the world. For, how could they have lived in their parents' houses, where there were so many children's mouths to feed?

It was then that a letter arrived from Sara, Hana's elder sister, the wife of the tinsmith. She invited the newlyweds to live with her in that big town, where they could learn a trade and find work.

And so it came to pass. Both girls now wrote to their parents two or three times a year, in the holidays, banal, stereotypical letters: 'Dear Parents, may you live to the age of one hundred and twenty! We are well, in good health, which is what we hope to hear from you and from our little brothers and sisters,' and so on.

But lately, new things had begun to slip into their letters. In her letters Hana, who had loved her father even more dearly ever since that night when Chaim recited the *gemara*, began ever more insistently to tell her parents to come and stay with them in their big city. She wrote that she knew how hard it was for them there in the village, and God forbid! she didn't want her father to wear himself out shoeing horses and her mother to wear herself out lugging milk to market… There were great opportunities in that big town of theirs. Life was easier and her little brothers and sisters would be able to go to school, they would be able to make a living more easily… She knew how to cajole her father!

At first, Schmiel the Blacksmith wouldn't hear of it; he batted away the very thought of it, like an annoying fly buzzing by his ear. But in time it began to niggle him. Particularly since in the meantime their life had grown even harder than it was when his daughter Hana had known it. There was little woodcutting in the forest now, the cartwheels rolled more seldom, the hoops wore out more slowly.

Most of the time, Schmiel sat under the roof of his lean-to smithy, his back resting against the fir-tree pole, and waited for hours on end, staring into space, the coals dead in the hearth, the bellows silent, without breath. Then, too, the grass had become sparse, the cow had grown thin and gave less milk.

And so it was that when a letter arrived from Hana, in which, after the usual opening of 'Dear Parents, may we all live to one hundred and twenty!' she added, 'Maybe Father would do well to come here first to see whether he likes it and then go back to fetch the rest of you,' this idea was a seed that found a ready-ploughed furrow. The whole night, Schmiel the Blacksmith was unable to sleep, nor did Rifka close her eyes, and near dawn she said to him, as if it were the most natural thing in the world, 'She's right, Schmiel, why don't you go and see?'

'*Folg mih a veig!*' snapped her husband. 'You say it as if it were just the same as my going to Dragomireşti, or Borscha, as if it were the same as popping over to Sighet…'

But it was plain he wasn't convinced of what he said.

And one sunny spring day – an ordinary work day – wearing his Sabbath clothes, his long grey overcoat, brushed to a sheen, and his wide-brimmed black hat, carrying a peasant knapsack, which contained his working clothes, a slab of maize bread, an onion, and some pastrami, Schmiel the Blacksmith left the village.

The villagers he met on the way shook his hand, wishing him a good journey. Rifka and the children walked with him to the end of the village, to the wooden bridge at the place where the Iza flows into the Tisza. There, Schmiel the Blacksmith kissed his wife, he kissed each of his children in turn, and departed.

Surrounded by the silent children, she stood for a long time in the middle of the road, by the bridge, watching as her husband's outline vanished around the bend in the road that led to Sighet station. Only then did she notice her eyes were wet. She dabbed them with a corner of her apron and softly said, 'Let's go home, children.'

A month passed, two months, three, and there was no word from Schmiel. Neither Rifka nor the rest of the village knew whether or not he would be coming back. Whether or not the rest of them would leave. Some of the neighbours, like Sura-Beile, who raised hens, like Malke, the grocer's wife, and other women from the village began to look at Rifka askance, they cast her pitying looks and heaved deep sighs after they passed. They began to think of her almost as an *aguna*, a woman who had lost her husband, but hadn't really lost him… a woman who had a husband, but didn't really have one… in short, a wretched situation.

Otherwise, nothing had changed. Rifka still went to town with the jugs of milk every morning; the children ate and grew the same as before, helping out in the house and in the garden as best they could. But the hearth in Schmiel's smithy remained cold, the bellows without breath; the hammer no longer clanged on the anvil, and no horse waited its turn, tethered to the pole, slowly chewing the armful of hay placed in front of it.

Who knows how many months passed like that until one day, an ordinary work day – except now it was autumn and it was raining – Schmiel the Blacksmith appeared in the village lane. He was dressed the same as when he had left, in his long grey overcoat and black broad-brimmed hat, except that instead of the peasant knapsack, he now had a polished cardboard suitcase and an umbrella tucked under his arm. A grey, heavy rain was pouring, and Schmiel held the umbrella tucked under his arm. It never crossed his mind to open it.

When the villagers saw him, men, women and children gathered around him in the rain, in the middle of the road, to greet him, to ask him what it had been like there, what he had seen, what he had done.

And without first going home, Schmiel the Blacksmith started talking. His leathery face, with its deep wrinkles that were never free of soot, now wore a slightly ironical, indulgent expression, like that of a man who had seen much, a man who secretly judged the rest of mankind, a man who was prepared to overlook many a thing.

Yes, the city was indeed big. Sighet was a little village in comparison. And the people there were different, they were strange, they rushed everywhere like madmen to make life as comfortable as possible… 'Imagine it, we walk miles and miles, as far as Dragomireşti, as Petrova, as Leordina, and even farther than that, whereas they wait a quarter of an hour for a tram so that they can go five hundred paces, in one of those wagons that moves without horses or a locomotive. It runs by itself along the tracks… We climb Siheiu Hill and Gruiu Hill and even higher than that, also on foot, but to climb to their houses on the upper floor, because most of the houses there are piled one on top of the other, they get into a little cage, they press a button, and the whole room, with all the people and their baggage in it, rises into the air as quick as can be, it made me feel queasy in the pit of my stomach, and I was always afraid that that hutch would break and I'd end up flying up into the sky… But after a while you get used to it. A man can get used to almost anything…'

'How are the children? His daughters, Sara and the beautiful Hana?' people asked.

'Very well, thank you. Sara's husband, Nahum, works on the roofs of the houses, fits sheet metal, makes drainpipes and gutters, and he earns quite good money. Hana and Moishe-Yankl's son Chaim iron neckties. Really! That's their job. Imagine it, they bring the neckties home to iron. I'd never have believed there'd be a need for so many neckties!' You could tell from the way he said it that Schmiel thought it a pointless occupation. That neckties themselves were pointless… 'But praise God, they earn an honest living.'

But why hadn't Schmiel stayed there? Why didn't he take the rest of his family there? A cloud passed across the soot-caked furrows of Schmiel's face and his voice grew solemn, grave. 'Why? Why? Because the whole time he stayed there, he had roamed the streets, the boulevards, the lanes, the alleys of that big city and nowhere had he found a smithy like his own… Nor had he seen any horse and cart… What could he do in a place where there were no horses or smithies?'

It was still raining, a slow, grey drizzle. With the suitcase in one hand and the umbrella tucked under his arm, Schmiel set off home to greet his wife and kiss his children's brows.

By that very afternoon, a number of horses were standing tethered in front of the smithy, slowly chewing clumps of hay, while Rifka worked the bellows, treading the board with one foot. To lend more weight to her foot, she pressed down on her knee with her hand. The coals glowed bright. And with the tongs Schmiel drew the red-hot iron from the fire and placed it on the anvil, he beat it with the hammer and rounded it into a beautiful shoe that was a perfect fit for the horse's hoof.

And the bright sparks flew in every direction…

At dawn one day in May 1944, the village was surrounded by tall, burly, moustached gendarmes, armed with machineguns, as if looking for violent malefactors. The Jews were rounded up from their one hundred and twenty houses and herded into the tradesmen's synagogue, where they sat huddled on the floor the whole night, their knees to their mouths, and the next morning they were taken to the goods ramp of Sighet station, loaded onto freight cars with planks and barbed wire nailed over the ventilation windows and heavy padlocks on the doors, and they were sent to Auschwitz.

Among them were Schmiel the Blacksmith, his wife Rifka, and their children. Schmiel was wearing his Sabbath clothes, his long grey overcoat, brushed to a sheen, his wide-brimmed black hat, and tucked under his arm he carried the umbrella he had received as a gift from Hana, his most beautiful daughter. He was white. His hair had turned white in the synagogue overnight, his face was as white as chalk, his wrinkles were still caked with the soot that never came out, although every Friday he took a sauna and then thrice plunged into the *mikva* water. He looked like a drawing in black ink, made by the hand of a master on chalked paper.

# The Scales

Hersch-Leib was a porter from an early age. 'I worked in transportation', he was later wont to say.

He was always cheerful, enterprising. Born into a farming family, with numerous siblings, he was never one to twiddle his thumbs waiting for his mother to put food on his plate. He went out to earn his own bread.

As a small child, he would leave the house before sunrise, so that he would arrive at Sighet market early. When he got there, he didn't hang around waiting for manna from heaven. As soon as he spotted a woman with a shopping basket, he would go up to her and ask whether she needed a porter and without waiting too long, he would grasp the basket. The lady would walk around the market stalls and booths, she would put a kilo of potatoes in the basket, half a kilo of onions, a few litres of beans, asking him all the while, 'Can you carry it, sonny? Isn't it too heavy?'

'Oh, no, it's not, madam, I can carry it and twice as much again!' he would say, stoutly hoisting the basket onto his shoulder. 'Buy as much as you like, madam!' he would add later, shifting the basket from one shoulder to the other.

In time, he began to have regular customers, not just occasional ones or those who appeared purely by chance. And a great deal of his work ran to a schedule. Especially on Wednesdays, which was market day, and Fridays, when the housewives did their shopping for Saturday. At seven in the morning, the basket of Mrs Friedman, the grocer's wife. At eight, the shopping of Mrs Hammer, the dentist's wife. Then came Mrs Steuer, the wine merchant's wife; Mrs Kraus, the apothecary's wife; Mrs Roda, the wife of the ear, nose and throat doctor; Mrs Moran, the lawyer's wife; and so on.

As is plain, he had rather a select clientele. This was also due to the fact that not only was Hersch-Leib polite, greeting the ladies with an 'I kiss your hand, madam' from a distance, not only was he eager to take their bags or baskets, but he was inventive. Which is to say, he reinvented the wheel. With the money he saved, he bought a wheel. After a while, he bought another wheel. Then, with a few pennies, he procured an old crate. He repaired it, reinforced it with nails, patched the holes with bits of old plank, wrapped it inside and out with blue paper, fitted a loop of string, and harnessed himself to it. In this way, he could pull up to three baskets if need be, even a sack of potatoes or up to twenty cabbages. The housewives knew they could rely on him.

Later, he bought himself a four-wheeled cart and a pony and delivered firewood to his customers' homes. After which he bought two horses, which allowed him to collect firewood from the source, which is to say, the forest, and take it to market; he was able to transport all manner of things and finally to marry and have children.

But at that point, ill fortune struck Hersch-Leib. Cutting wood in the forest, loading and unloading logs, was not an easy job and he would have very much liked his firstborn to be a boy. It was a girl. Then another girl. The third time, his wife bore yet another girl. And then another.

Hersch-Leib then lifted his eyes to heaven, like Job, thanked the Lord for what He had given him, and abandoned any further attempts.

But what came to pass? The Lord Above does not sit idle, but has a thousand ways to compensate a man and even to reward him if He so wishes.

Haya, his eldest daughter, had grown up to be tall and lanky like her father. From an early age, she showed no interest in housework. She didn't want to sweep, to wash dishes, to peel potatoes. On the other hand, she had a great love of horses. She groomed them, she climbed up into the hayloft and with a pitchfork tossed down fodder into their mangers, she drew water from the well and poured it into the troughs for them to drink. When Hersch-Leib was busy elsewhere, she would take the reins and drive the cart. Almost without anybody realising it, the young girl went into 'transportation' just like her father.

Haya had even come to an understanding with her father: he was to pay her for her work cash in hand, the same as he would any stranger. Hersch-Leib should not pay her more because she was his daughter, but nor should he pay her less.

And like her father before her, Haya saved up her money to buy a wheel, then another, then another two, then a cart, a horse, a second horse, thus entering the ranks of the serious carters. She wore a sheepskin jerkin and opanci on her feet, just like they did, and her skirt and headscarf bothered the men not at all.

The carters had made Haya and Hersch-Leib their own. Drummer's Ion, thus named because his father had used to beat the drum around the village, calling, 'Be it known that the tax is due,' and Trustworthy's Gheorghe, thus named because his father was village watchman and you could have faith in him, and Simion's Petru, and all the other village carters were accustomed to that carter girl, a slender pine sapling, which demanded sun, air, and water like all the other pines.

At the time, they had started felling the beech forest on the hill above Siheiu, and two-horse carts had been hired to transport the timber to the lumberyard in town.

Before the break of day, the carts set off from the village, and you could see the file of lamps climbing the hill to the forest. Late at night, the carts descended with their loads. It was difficult work, especially in autumn, after heavy rainfall or sleet, when the road became muddy and slippery. Then you would hear the drawn-out shouts in the night:

'Hey, Ion, put on the brakes, slippery ro-o-oad…'

Then the voice of Drummer's Ion:

'Hey, Hersch-Leib, put on the brakes, slippery ro-o-oad…'

then the voice of Simion's Petru:

'Hey, Haya, put on the brakes, slippery ro-o-oad…'

Then the girl's voice:

'Hey, Gheo, put on the brakes, slippery ro-o-oad…'

And so on.

And the long file of lamps could be seen twinkling in the night, descending the hill.

Cart, horses, wheels, brakes – all well and good, but time was passing and Haya, tall and lanky as she was, as thin as a plank, was starting to develop curves that filled out her clothes. There was no doubt about it: the time had come for her to marry.

Nor were Hersch-Leib's other daughters standing still. They were ripening too, and their time was coming with rapid steps, even a blind man could see that. Ever since that incident of old, involving our ancestor Jacob and Laban's daughters, Leah and Rachel, it's been known that girls need to be married off as soon as they come of age, though not just any old how, God forbid. Many things might be said of Laban, that he was a profiteer and a trickster, that he deceived poor Jacob, making him work fourteen years for his two daughters, but the one thing you can't say is that he wasn't an excellent father and that he didn't take care to marry off his daughters.

Hersch-Leib's Haya was a difficult case, however. Far more difficult than Laban's Leah, perhaps. Not that she was ugly. If you regarded her closely, she was actually very pleasant to look at: green eyes, dark, arching eyebrows… But when did she have time to stand still so that you could get a good look at her? And more to the point, who would want to get a good look at her? She was a tomboy who talked to the horses and the boys didn't pay her much attention.

What was needed, therefore, was a push from elsewhere. And during her sleepless nights, lying in her bed in the dark, the girl's mother, Brana, a tall, fat, energetic woman, would nag her husband in the next bed: 'What kind of father are you, Hersch-Leib? What are you going to do about Haya? You forget that you have four daughters, long life to them! Four daughters to marry! Or do you want my daughters to grow old here at home, God forbid! Tell me, husband, what is it you want?'

'I want to go to sleep, Brana,' he moaned, 'it's the middle of the night.'

'At night you want to sleep, in the day you don't have time, tell-me-what-you're-going-to-do-about-our-Haya, what-do-you-want-for-her-to-remain-unmarried, God forbid, I'll-let-you-sleep-as-long-as-you-like-if-you-tell-me, damned husband, it-would-have-been-better-if-I'd-never-met-you, or-if-I'd-broken-both-my-legs-before-I-passed-under-the-canopy-with-you…'

On hearing his wife's objurgations, spoken almost in a single breath, Hersch-Leib turned on his side in bed and said, 'What do you want from me, woman? What should I do? Go out in the street with an axe, catch a suitor and drag him back?'

'No, but why don't you do what other men do? Why don't you talk to Reb Motl-Shadkhan? Good suitors for so many girls he's found. He can't find one for our Haya too?'

'Very well, I'll talk to Reb Motl-Shadkhan,' muttered Hersch-Leib placatingly. Then he then turned over and within moments he was fast asleep, snoring.

The next day, Hersch-Leib rode his cart to Sighet and sought out Reb Motl, the marriage broker, who was famous because, although marriages were made in heaven, as was well known, the more difficult cases were nonetheless entrusted to him to solve here on earth.

It was a Thursday evening. Hersch-Leib found the red-headed, one-eyed, hunchbacked matchmaker bent over a large tome of the Gemara, dozing. When the rather embarrassed Hersch-Leib told him what it was all about, Reb Motl had a flash of inspiration. Even before Hersh-Leib could finish speaking, Reb Motl cried out: 'Yumi Alter!'

'What? Yumi Alter?' asked the carter in amazement.

'His name is Benyumin Alter. Everybody calls him Yumi. He's a *yeshive-bucher* orphan. He studies at the Yeshivah here in Sighet and lives in lodgings. This very day I tested him. You know, every Thursday, the students are examined on what they have learned during the week. He has a head, that boy...'

Hersch-Leib listened to him open-mouthed.

'A *yeshive-bucher* for my daughter? Do you know my daughter?'

'I know every marriageable girl and boy in Sighet and in every village in the Tisza, Iza, Mara and Vişeu valleys!' replied Reb Motl, slightly offended.

'But Reb Motl, an impoverished, orphaned yeshivah student for my daughter?' said Hersch-Leib, indignant. 'My daughter has a dowry, God be praised, she has a cart and two horses, she has money saved. Why don't you propose a young man who's well off?'

'A young man who's well off, a young man who's well off,' muttered Reb Motl into his pointed, flame-red beard. 'The rich man wants a boy who's well off and the poor man wants a boy who's well off. As if I were running a factory that turned out Rothschilds... What about the boys who aren't well off? They're supposed to remain bachelors all their lives?'

After his anger subsided a little, the *shadkhan* continued more calmly.

'Not so fast, Hersch-Leib. Let us consider. Let's say I find your daughter a rich man, who after the wedding goes bankrupt and loses his entire fortune. You even find you have to pay off his debts… Such things have been known to happen… What then? Better you find her a boy who's already poor, but with a good head on his shoulders, who will be able to become somebody… Maybe he'll take up trade and become rich. Maybe he'll learn a profitable trade. And who knows, with that head of his, maybe he'll become a famous rabbi and people from all over the world will come to ask his advice…'

There followed a moment of silence. Hersch-Leib scratched the back of his neck, not knowing what to reply. On seeing him waver, Reb Motl marshalled his most persuasive argument: 'In the end, what does it cost you to meet him, Hersch-Leib? Look, I'll come with him to your synagogue in Chebliţe on the Sabbath and after prayers, you'll invite him to your house for dinner, like any other wayfarer passing through your village… But the young ones must know nothing about it. Don't tell your daughter anything about what we have discussed, and I'll not say anything to the boy. We'll see… God is a father…'

The carter nodded dumbly. What did he have to lose if he met him?

And that Sabbath, the yeshivah student from Sighet was shyly sitting on the edge of his seat at the table of Hersch-Leib. Haya was looking in amazement at that tall, thin young man with the long neck and protuberant Adam's apple, with the long, pale face, in which glittered two large, dark eyes, eyes unusually large and dark. He was wearing a round black hat with a wide brim, a shirt of thick cloth, but clean and white, buttoned to the neck, without a tie, and a buttoned-up coat, rather worn in the elbows, which reached to his knees and from beneath which poked the legs of coarse-cloth trousers, down to his white socks and black, down-at-heel, but well-polished shoes.

Later, the young guest recited the Kiddush, the prayer to bless the wine, with his eyes closed, holding the glass in his hand. He had beautiful white hands with long, slender fingers. Then, after the meal, he intoned the *zemirot*, the Sabbath song. He had a warm, pleasant voice.

What a pity he was so poor, thought Hersch-Leib. What a pity... But who knows? Perhaps... Stranger things had happened in this world... Reb Motl knew what he was talking about. He had arranged many marriages.

After the meal was over, it wasn't clear who had arranged it, perhaps Brana, the girl's mother, perhaps it just turned out that way, but Haya and Yumi found themselves alone on the bench on the porch. It was a warm midsummer's day. The other three girls had gone for a walk. Hersch-Leib went to take a nap on the couch, and Brana remained seated at the table to read the *Tseno Ureno*. But her mind was not on her reading, for she kept peeking outside, through the dining room window, to see what was happening on the porch. Brana had no reason to worry, however. The two young ones were sitting quietly. Haya at one end of the bench, Yumi at the other. They were talking. Or rather Yumi was talking, without looking at the girl, and Haya was listening to him in amazement. Never had she heard such things.

'Have you ever thought about the way in which this world is made? How life is made?'

The girl looked at him in amazement. Ever since she was little, she had thought about horses, hay, carts, timber, about feeding, watering, grooming the horses, about carting timber from the forest to the town, about how to brake the cart on a muddy slope, about how to earn her daily bread. She had thought about many other things, but never about how the world and how life was made. It made her feel dizzy.

'There is the heaven and the earth, dry land and water, huge trees and frail blades of grass, animals and people … and there are people tall and short, strong and weak, beautiful and ugly, healthy and sick … And all of them live …'

'What else could they do?' asked Haya. She felt like laughing out loud at that fantastically obvious idea, but she didn't dare.

'You see, I have discovered something … How to live … Oh, it's not so simple …' whispered Yumi, his large dark eyes shining more brightly than ever in his chalk-white face. 'People are not happy or unhappy, as they believe, or as we believe they believe … If one has something or lacks something, another has something else or lacks something else … Or both one and the same man has that something and that something else …'

The girl cast a strange look at that white profile. She didn't understand a thing. Yumi felt her eyes on his right cheek.

'There is a pair of scales, which swing up and down, up and down, but always regain their balance … Otherwise, it would be impossible to live … I'm not thinking of the Lord Above weighing our good and bad deeds … Which our fellow men also see, and by which they judge us … I'm talking about a different pair of scales, the inner scales … It's hard to understand. Not even I understand it very well yet. It's even harder to explain in words … But I think about it a lot …'

Yumi fell silent for a few moments, then went on, without turning to look back at the girl.

'I have a friend at the yeshivah, my best friend. He is humpbacked, the poor boy, he has a hump like a sack of potatoes on his back … Well, what do you think? Am I happier than he is?'

'Naturally you are!' the girl hastened to reply.

'That's what I thought too. When things were hard for me, I used to say to myself: Shut up! Don't complain! Don't sin before the Lord! But now, I'm not so sure … I look at him every day, I see how he lives, how happy he is, how sad he is, how he eats, how he fasts … Well, I don't see any difference. He is not unhappier than

I am or anyone else is… Maybe because he doesn't see himself with my eyes or anybody else's eyes. But with his own eyes… you understand?'

'No, I don't,' replied Haya, categorically.

'If he could see himself with my eyes, he wouldn't be able to bear his life. Nor would we, if we had a different kind of seeing, be able to bear seeing him live like that… He must have something, something very precious, something inside him that compensates him. Something that weighs heavily on the other pan of the scales… In one pan, the humpback, in the other, something… something just as heavy…'

'What exactly?'

'I don't know! I'm going to try to find out. But there must be something inside him, in his soul, in his head… A strength, a power that makes him move through this world the same as you or I do, which makes him laugh the same as we do, cry the same as we do… which makes him able to be as unhappy or as happy, depending on the case, just like other people…'

Yumi was speaking more and more passionately.

'Yes, there is a pair of scales, a balance between a man's bodily strengths and weaknesses. If he is deaf, he can read lips. If he is blind, he has sharper hearing. The one-armed man's arm is stronger and the one-legged man's leg is stronger… There is a balance between the soul's virtues and vices, between evil and good, between happiness and sadness, between gentleness and anger… And between what is called good and bad fortune… All things are compensated… just as there is a balance between the bodily and the spiritual. The cripple has greater spiritual strength. Perhaps also greater endurance of suffering… The pans of the scales swing up and down, up and down, now one is higher, the other lower, now one is lower, the other higher, creating disequilibrium… But they always balance in the end… Otherwise, life wouldn't be possible. And there is a huge, a giant pair of scales that holds the whole world in balance…'

Yumi suddenly lowered his voice, imparting a secret.

'I'm going to write a book about it ... *The Scales of Life.*' And he repeated the title a few more times, listening to it as if it were a strain of music. '*The Scales of Life ... The Scales of Life ...*'

Then, turning toward the girl for the first time, he said:

'But don't tell anybody until the book is ready!'

And Yumi's pale, translucent cheek abruptly turned pink.


Benyumin Alter's book, *The Scales of Life*, was never published.

Nor did Yumi and Haya ever marry.

But Reb Motl-Shadkhan was not to blame for that.

Probably it had not been decided in heaven and so all the wisdom, understanding and skill of Reb Motl were in vain.

Although Haya had thought a lot about that frail young man with his head in the clouds and his strange scales, like a child's innocent plaything ...

Although Yumi thought about her too, more than he would have allowed himself, about the tall, lanky, healthy girl, who trod so heavily, who had both feet so firmly on the ground, and who was so awkward in her silk Sabbath dress ...

Nonetheless, nothing was decided up there, in heaven.

Perhaps because the very hand that ought to have written the next chapter in the book of Haya and Yumi's life began to tremble, the pen fell from that hand and the page, barely begun, remained blank.

For here on earth, the spring of 1944 came and life began to hurtle like a cart without brakes down a steep, muddy hill.

Along with the one hundred and twenty Jewish families from the village, Hersch-Leib, the carter, who had worked all his life in 'transportation', and his wife Brana and four daughters were taken from their house and driven to the tradesmen's synagogue, where they spent the night. The next day, they were herded into a column and, guarded by gendarmes with cockerel feathers in their caps, they were marched to the goods ramp of Sighet Station, loaded into cattle trucks with planks and barbed wire nailed over the ventilation windows, and sent to Auschwitz.

Before leaving the house, Haya had gone up into the hayloft and tossed down fodder into the horses' mangers.

The next day, on the goods ramp of Sighet Station, where the Jews were counted into the cattle trucks, Haya thought to glimpse the pale face and shining dark eyes of Yumi Alter a few trucks down. But she wasn't sure. There were so many pale faces there, and so many dark eyes, shining with fever.

The count went on monotonously.

Thirty-one… thirty-two… thirty-three…

Haya climbed up into the cattle truck. There, in the semi-darkness, in the crush, strange questions arose in her mind for the first time: What has happened to the scales of life? What has happened to the large scales that hold the world in balance?

In the cattle truck next to her there was nobody able to answer the question.

# Fear

Chaim Rives was afraid of nothing. He was afraid of neither hard work, nor illness, nor the bad dogs in people's yards, nor dreams, nor ill omens. There was only one thing alone of which he was terribly afraid: tomorrow. To be exact, he was afraid he might not have anything to eat tomorrow. He gladly endured hunger today, so long as he knew that tomorrow he would have something to eat.

This fear probably came from childhood, when he had never had enough to eat. His mother was a washerwoman with a large number of children and a large amount of laundry to wash. He couldn't remember his father. Nor did his mother ever speak to him or the other children about their father: Maybe she had forgotten, maybe she didn't have the time, maybe there was no point.

His mother was called Rive and the children were named after her. He was Rive's Chaim. It was unknown how many older siblings he had, since some had died in infancy, some had grown up and then been scattered throughout the world, and nobody had kept count or track of them.

The fact is that Chaim Rives wandered the world alone, unafraid of bad dogs, illness, dreams or ill omens, unafraid of anything except tomorrow.

That was why he did not wait for tomorrow in his mother's ramshackle house, in which he had remained the sole tenant, he did not wait for her with folded arms to come home and catch him unawares, but always went to meet her on her way back. He wandered from house to house, through the villages and the outskirts of towns, he opened doors, stood on thresholds, without uttering a word. And the women of those houses sometimes gave him odd jobs to do, but more often they gave him a leaden penny with a hole in the middle or a crust of bread.

But sometimes there would be a stern woman who did not yet know him and she would yell at the man standing wordlessly in her doorway: 'Have you no shame? A grown man going begging at people's doors!'

It was true: besides making Chaim Rives dirt poor, God had also cursed him with a perfect health that was plain to see. He was broad in the back, brawny, and he had a round, tanned face. He did not try to conceal it or to feign otherwise. He did not evince infirmities that he did not possess, he did not bandage his arm, he did not limp, he did not put on dark glasses.

'For a strong man like you not to work!'

'Give me work,' Chaim would answer, without a trace of offence in his voice.

He was honest. As a matter of fact, he had started out in life as an itinerant labourer. He had done everything, but he had never learned a trade; he was therefore skilled at everything and nothing. And he did anything: he lugged water from the well, chopped wood, nailed fences, stacked hay. He did not refuse any job, hard or easy, and it was only his fear of tomorrow, which had dwelled in his soul ever since he was a little boy, that made him accept a small leaden penny with a hole in it instead of work, a penny that was almost worthless by itself and only began to be worth something when joined with many other such pennies.

'Give me work! I'll do anything!'

The housewife would feel embarrassed. She had not been expecting such a reply. She had not thought it anything to do with her. She only meant that he should go and look for work somewhere else. But what if everybody sent him to look somewhere else? And what the hell could she give him to do? Her husband chopped the wood; her daughters lugged water from the well. And if she put him to work, it would cost her coins without holes in them, whereas like this she could get rid of him at the price of a crust of bread or a worthless penny.

Chaim saved up those worthless pennies. He then exchanged them for coins without holes in them, he exchanged the coins for small banknotes, the small banknotes for large banknotes, which he smoothed nicely and hid under his patched mattress.

Chaim Rives never thought about getting married, although he too had been young once, and although he could have found a woman as solitary as he, a wanderer like him, with whom to save worthless pennies, it would have meant two mouths to feed, and then there would have been children and he was afraid, he had a terrible fear of tomorrow. That was why he remained alone. That was why he never ate his fill today, but saved up coins with holes in them and gradually exchanged them for banknotes that he smoothed and hid under the mattress. He never looked at them, he never got up in the middle of the night to count them secretly, he was merely content to have them, he slept soundly knowing that they were there, that he could take them from under the mattress at any time and buy something to eat with them, buy a coat to cover his body, buy some firewood to warm himself in winter. For he was not a miser, a man who loved money, rather he was simply afraid of tomorrow and day after day, year after year, he kept saving that paper money, endlessly, because life is made in such a way that a man cannot know in advance how many tomorrows he will have.

And so, Chaim Rives never had any dealings with the registry office. He never married, he never had children. Others went to the registry office on his behalf, and even then, only twice, each time when he was powerless and unaware: once when he was born, and the second time after he died. When he came into this world, a neighbour would have reluctantly gone to announce the birth of yet another child to Rive. Nobody kept count of how many had come into this world. Or maybe they will have forgotten to announce the birth, or maybe the clerk will have misheard and made the entry under the wrong name, which is why Chaim Rives was not conscripted during either the First or the Second World War. And after he left this world, the authorities of course took care to register the death, without very many details, since nobody knew more than that he was Chaim Rives and that he had been born and recently died.

That was how things turned out, for on that day in the month of May 1944, when the Jews of the village were rounded up at the synagogue and then sent to Auschwitz in cattle trucks, the gendarmes pounded with their rifle butts on the door of Chaim Rives's hovel at the bottom of the hill. But nobody answered. They broke the door down, they entered, and they found the aforementioned Chaim Rives lying on an old patched mattress, with a serene, almost happy smile on his face. To the two gendarmes it seemed as if he were smiling mockingly. How dare a filthy Jew like him smile like that to their faces?

He was summarily buried in the Jewish graveyard on the side of the hill; nobody knows where, since there was no grave marker.

The gendarmes and the notary's assistant made an inventory: a table, a chair, a bed, a mattress. And under the mattress, wads of banknotes of every size and colour: Austro-Hungarian coronas from the time of Franz-Josef, roubles issued under Tsar Nicholas, and all sorts of banknotes that once circulated in that region at the end of the last century. Wads of banknotes, crisp, smoothed by long years of sleep, but worthless, having long since been withdrawn from circulation.

# Three Rolls
# for a Penny

Finding himself in town on business and feeling hungry, Avram Eizicovitch went into a bread shop to buy something to eat. One of today's rolls, that is, one taken fresh from the oven that morning, cost a penny. But for the same penny you could buy three harder rolls, that is, three left over from yesterday or the day before.

And Avram Eizicovitch bought three hard rolls from yesterday or the day before. Not because he was poor, God forbid. The folk from his village said he was as rich as the Korah from the Bible, while the more modern folk from town said he was the village Croesus. And all of them were of the opinion that not even he himself knew how wealthy he was. Which was completely wrong. For, in the inside pocket of his threadbare coat Avram Eizicovitch always kept a dog-eared grey notebook, full of figures, symbols, and sums intelligible to him alone. He knew exactly what he owned, how much he owned, where he owned it.

He had started out with nothing thirty years before. A small plot of land next to a wooden house with a shingle roof, where he lived even now, which Fradl had brought as a dowry, and a few large banknotes which he had saved while he still lived in the house of his father, who was also a hard-working villager. From an early age Avram had known how to do sums, and now he knew where he had a patch of forest, where he had land for ploughing, where he had pastures in the mountains, he knew how many milk cows he had and how much milk each gave, he knew how many sheep he had up at the sheepfold and how much cheese each ewe produced, how much wool each sheep gave.

As his wealth increased, so did the number of his children. Or was it that the number of his children increased with the area of the land he owned? Avram Eizicovitch didn't stop to wonder. Idle questions were never his style… He was convinced that his offspring were the gift of God in Heaven, just as his wealth was the result of his hard work, his temperance, his health, his endurance, all of which are also ultimately gifts of the Almighty.

Avram Eizicovitch and Fradl, his wife, were gifted with eight children, five boys and three girls: Chaim and Jossi, after whom Dvora, their eldest daughter came into the world, then Leizer and Beri, after which arrived the other two girls, Ressi and Hana, and finally Moti, the youngest. And as they grew, each found work on the farm, work came as naturally to them as breathing the air or drinking water; the boys dug and reaped and ploughed, and the girls cleaned the house, cooked, darned socks, milked and curried the cows in the barn. The children grew and the parcels of forest and fields for ploughing multiplied. Lord God, it is a great blessing *naches fun kinder*, that is, for the Lord Above to give you good, hardworking children who are healthy and sound of mind.

But there was one of them, the youngest to be exact, who showed some strange attitudes. Moti wasn't interested in ploughing, or harvesting apples, or selling grain – Avram had been planning to buy a house in town and to open there a grain and fruit store – none of that interested the youngest son. Moti wanted to become a doctor. And Fradl, Avram's wife, was beside herself with joy: 'Yes, yes, may God grant he become a doctor!' She could already picture herself as the mother of a doctor. How silly women can be sometimes! And Avram Eizicovitch, with his pencil and his dog-eared grey notebook in front of him, tried to explain things to her. True, everybody would respectfully greet him, address him as doctor, doff their hats, it would be doctor this, doctor that… all very nice, no denying it, a great honour, but if you looked at it more closely, what was a doctor in fact? How much did a doctor earn? A man who knows how to hold a pencil and do simple arithmetic isn't fooled so easily… Look at the doctor in our village, for example: for a measly twenty he has to go all over the place, he has to travel to the nastiest places… And if you send him five eggs or half a hen, he can't thank you enough… And then just look at what it's like in town, weak-minded woman that you are. There are forty-odd doctors there. Five of them are well off, they have their own houses and it's said they earn good money, how much they earn, I don't know, because I haven't counted their money. Another ten make a living, and the rest barely scrape by… But can I talk to you? The lad is still young and daft, he hasn't even started primary school, and already he wants to be a doctor. Now Fradl was a stupid woman, when explained to her, she nodded her head and said, 'Yes, yes, husband, you're right,' but in the depths of her heart, she still wanted to be the mother of a doctor. A great blessing indeed to have *naches fun kinder,* for your children to bring you joy.

But the whole story has no point whatsoever, firstly because it has nothing to do with the three stale rolls Avram Eizicovitch bought, and secondly because regardless of his mother's willingness and his father's lack thereof, Moti, the youngest son, was unfortunately never to become a doctor.

So Avram Eizicovitch reckoned that three stale rolls were better than one fresh roll, no matter how crusty and tempting. And if you have good teeth, and he did, thank God, three rolls are more filling than one. Even a chucklehead knew that. He paid for the three stale rolls with a copper penny and left the shop.

In the street, he began to munch one of the rolls. Whenever he came into town on business – he used to travel there in Chaim-Leib's cart or else he would go by train, third class, since there wasn't a fourth class – whenever he came into town, his principle was 'haggle hard, pay honestly', which is to say, get the lowest price you can, but pay honestly once you've made the bargain. Or else he would come to pay his taxes; 'what belongs to the state, belongs to the state', he would say, and taxes had to be paid on time and to the last penny. When he came into town, he never entered a restaurant or a bodega or a public house to eat. That was pure conceitedness, vanity, stupidity, and above all a pointless expense: to sit pompously at a table waiting for a smiling, dapper waiter to come and serve you, when you could just as easily serve yourself, with your own hands, after all, you're not a cripple, God forbid, and you can eat a packed lunch on a bench in the park or munch a roll in the street, as he was doing now.

He stopped in front of a shop window and gazed for a long moment, smiling scornfully at the life-size mannequins: cardboard female mannequins with painted cheeks, tall and with slender waists, dressed in expensive, gaudy silk dresses, cardboard male mannequins with red, made-up faces, dressed in impeccably tailored suits of fine cloth, in trousers with razor-sharp creases, mannequins wearing neckties, shawls, mannequins with handbags and cufflinks of every colour and size. 'Elegant' read the sign above the shop window. What vanity, good God! He, Avram Eizicovitch, had a set of clothes for everyday wear and a set for the Sabbath. And his wife Fradl likewise had two dresses, one of which was for the Sabbath, and two aprons, two headscarves, two pairs of shoes, and so on. And their five sons and three daughters likewise. What was the point of so much expensive silk and cloth? Avram Eizicovitch stood in front of the shop window and he simply couldn't understand it. All of it seemed designed purely to take the money out of a man's pocket. It's a known fact that a man can't eat with two spoons at once, and you cover your nakedness with only a single coat at a time, and with a clean one on the Sabbath, why would you need ten or twenty sets of clothes hanging in your cupboard? And what's more, with one spoon or two, with one coat or ten, we all end up in the same place.

And as he gazed at that shop window of vanities, sunk in thought, something unbelievable happened, something ridiculous, something almost outrageous. There was a loud bang, the sound of breaking glass, and the window of the Elegant haberdashery exploded into fragments. Had he wished, he could now have reached out and felt the silk and the cloth that garbed the shop dummies. But Avram Eizicovitch was in no mood for that.

What had happened? Standing in front of the window, he had tried to take a bite of the hard roll, which refused to yield, and when it snapped abruptly in his mouth, he had struck the window with his elbow, loudly shattering it.

You had to buy three hard rolls, Avram, three for a penny, didn't you? You made a saving, but now it's going to cost you dearly, he thought. And no sooner had he thought that than the shopkeeper ran outside and, seeing a man in shabby clothes, a small, puny man in a greasy, faded black hat, with a haphazardly trimmed ginger beard, he grabbed him by the arm lest he run away and yelled, 'You broke my window! You're paying for that! You're not leaving till you've paid!'

Avram Eizicovitch looked at the shopkeeper wide-eyed, as if he had fallen from the moon. What? it flashed through his mind. He, Avram Eizicovitch, should pay? For what? For nothing. He should pay without receiving anything in return? A completely pointless expense? It was ridiculous. It was outrageous. It was absurd. He'd never encountered anything like it in his life. Never in his life had he squandered so much as a single penny, nor was he about to start now. He jerked his arm from the grasp of the owner of the Elegant haberdashery.

'Have no fear, I'm not going to run away and leave you with a broken window!' he said proudly.

'That window costs three hundred!' said the shopkeeper angrily.

Rather than reply, Avram carefully examined the front of the building, as if measuring the width, height, breadth of the walls, counting the windows and chimneys. It was rather a smart building, with an upper storey, located quite near the centre of town.

'Whose is this house?'

'What's it to you?' asked the proprietor of the haberdashery, astounded.

'Where does the owner of the house live?'

'On the upper floor, but what's it to you? It's me you have to pay! I'm the tenant, the proprietor of the shop!'

But by then Avram Eizicovitch had entered the courtyard and was climbing the stairs. The proprietor of the haberdashery stood waiting to catch him when he came back down.

After about half an hour, Eizicovitch descended, took three large folded banknotes from his pocket and handed them to the shopkeeper.

'Repair the window! But mind you do a good job!' he said, and then went out into the street. He looked the building up and down once more, this time with different eyes, with the eyes of a property owner, and then took the half-eaten roll out of his pocket and carried on gnawing. He was devilishly hungry.

The proprietor of the Elegant haberdashery stood holding the money in bewilderment. It was only later that he discovered that Avram Eizicovitch had bought the whole building, upper-floor apartments, ground-floor shop, shop window, everything. Only then had it suited him to pay for the repairs. It was now his house.

When in 1944 they confiscated first his grazing meadows in the mountains, and then his fields for ploughing, and then his cattle shed, and then his flock of sheep at the sheepfold, and then that building with the upper storey and the Elegant haberdashery on the ground floor, and finally that old, modest house made of oak beams, with a shingle roof, in which he had lived for more than thirty years, they did so legally, with signed and stamped documents from the town hall, and Avram Eizicovitch couldn't understand a thing. His whole life he had toiled, along with Fradl, his wife, and their eight children, with Chaim and Jossi, with Dvora, their eldest daughter, and then with Leizer and Beri, with Ressi and Hana, and with Moti, the youngest; he had toiled and saved, he had worn a single threadbare coat on work days and a black suit on the Sabbath, and Fradl had had just two dresses, two aprons, two headscarves, and the children had had no more than two sets of clothes, two pairs of shoes, two shirts, and so on. In his entire life he had never set foot in a restaurant or a bodega or a public house, dapper, smiling waiters had not served him, but rather he had eaten three stale penny rolls instead of one fresh, crusty roll. And now he couldn't understand a thing.

Nor could he understand a thing when those gendarmes, with cockerel feathers in their caps, armed with machineguns and spare magazines, led him away with Fradl and their children to the town ghetto, after which, a few weeks later, they were taken to the station goods ramp and loaded into one of the cattle trucks with planks and barbed wire nailed over the ventilation windows.

And he couldn't understand a thing when he arrived on that smooth path between barbed-wire fences and white posts, with the searchlights shining in his eyes, and somebody hoarsely shouted for the men to separate from the women, and he went one way with the boys, with Chaim and Jossi and Leizer and Beri and Moti, the youngest, who had wanted to become a doctor, and Fradl went the other way with the girls, with Dvora and Ressi and Hana, until they vanished in the crowd, until he lost sight of them. And he went with the boys until an officer in a black uniform pointed him to the left.

And Avram Eizicovitch went in the direction he was pointed, he went with his sons, who didn't want to part with their father, he went without understanding a thing, not a single thing.

# Matriarchy

In all his nineteen years, Roni Dreispan had entered the living room only once.

His mother, Mrs Relly Dreispan, was a small, energetic woman, as restless as quicksilver. By the front door, she had placed a number of pairs of slippers and in summer she would say to her husband and son, 'Don't come in wearing your shoes, because you'll bring all the dust inside the house!'

And in winter, she would say, 'Don't come in wearing your boots, because you'll bring all the mud inside the house!'

Which was absurd, because even had they wanted to, the two men wouldn't have been able to bring all the dust or all the mud inside the house, but only a tiny part of all the dust and mud that there was. But that was Relly Dreispan for you. She exaggerated. Her husband, Daniel Dreispan, a mountain of a man, and her son, Aron, whose pet name was Roni, and who was as large as his father, obeyed that small, thin woman with pale eyes and a nondescript face, a face which it was impossible to say whether it was beautiful or ugly, and who wore her hair piled in a tall bun on the top of her head.

Even with the tall bun, Mrs Relly was still no taller than the shoulders of her husband and son, but in their house, she gave the orders, she ruled. Or rather, she reigned.

She toiled like a slave and reigned like an absolute monarch. She cooked the food, darned the socks, washed the dishes, cleaned and tidied the house so that even with a magnifying glass, you wouldn't have been able to find a single speck of dust. She would place the slippers in a neat row by the front door and when her husband came home from work – he worked as a cabinetmaker at a workshop in the neighbourhood, not far away – and when her son came home from school, they would take their shoes off at the front door and enter the house in slippers.

There were also a few pairs of spare slippers by the front door, in case of visitors. Whoever wanted to see the slippers would see them. He would take off his shoes and put on the slippers. And whoever didn't want to see them or who didn't notice them would come in off the street wearing his shoes. Mrs Relly, the mistress of the house, would take note of every step he made and after he left, she would quickly wipe the footprints off the floor using a damp cloth, usually muttering something about upbringing and manners.

As is plain by now, Mrs Relly Dreispan's house was in fact a kind of temple. A temple of cleanliness! You entered only after performing a certain rite. And the same as in any self-respecting temple, her house had its holy of holies, a sanctum you entered neither barefoot nor in slippers, but only on rare occasions, on the highest holidays: the dining room.

The Dreispan family home was quite poky; other than the dining room, it consisted of the parents' bedroom and Roni's little room, but even so, they never entered that dining room the size of a dance-hall and they never ate there.

Only Mrs Relly, the mistress of the house, entered the dining room. Every morning, after carefully washing her feet, she would enter barefoot, lock the door behind her and, the high priestess of cleanliness, officiate the rites: she would wipe the dust from the old mahogany furniture, she would wipe the silverware and porcelain in the sideboard, the crystal vases on the large, solid-wood table, in the corners she would polish the dark brown floor with wax, she would wipe the thick red and blue velvet carpet with a damp cloth, and then she would tiptoe barefoot out of that large, silent room, locking the door behind her, after which nobody else would enter: 'At least I'm able to keep the dining room clean,' Mrs Relly would say, with a deep sigh.

And for years at a time, nobody else set foot in that spacious room, as large as a school dancehall. The occasion would have had to be rare indeed, it would have had to be unique, or festive.

And such an occasion arose only once in the young life of Roni Dreispan. That occasion was the engagement of Hanna, Mrs Relly's younger sister. There were three daughters, Relly, Hanna and Lilly. Their parents were old and lived in a little house at the edge of town, where it would have been impossible to hold Hanna's engagement. Especially since Hanna had found an excellent match. Her fiancé was a rich grain merchant, a fine man, as good as warm bread. Later, not long after the wedding, it transpired that he wasn't a merchant, but only a sort of go-between, that he didn't trade in grain, but only bran, that he wasn't rich, but hoped to pay off his debts with his wife's dowry, and that he wasn't so fine and good; wagging tongues even went so far as to hint that he used to raise his hand to her for nothing at all. But all these things couldn't have been known beforehand, a marriage is like *cholent*, as they say, you put it in the oven and you don't know how it will turn out, and the engagement party was held in Mrs Relly Dreispan's dining room, and there was great merriment and rejoicing, and in a surge of largesse, Relly promised to hold the engagement party for Lilly, her youngest sister, in the dining room too.

Roni was five years old at the time, and that large, spacious dining room, with its tall ceiling, its dark red solid mahogany sideboard, its high-backed chairs upholstered in red leather, its shiny crockery, its clinking glasses, its candles flickering in their silver sticks, its soft velvet carpet in which your feet sank deeply, all those things enchanted and bewitched him, and in his mind the boy prayed to God that his Aunt Lilly's engagement would arrive quickly.

But the engagement did not arrive. Perhaps because Lilly was more exacting and was able to choose as she pleased among numerous eligible suitors, or perhaps there were not so many suitors for her to choose from, or perhaps the family had become more cautious, or perhaps it was simply fated to be, or perhaps Lilly's name was not written in the book of marriages kept in heaven, but the fact is that she was never to be betrothed, either in Relly's dining room or anywhere else.

And so it was that Roni never set foot in that room again. When nobody was looking, he would look through the keyhole, straining to cram as much as he could within his field of vision; he would glimpse a corner of the sideboard, with its silverware and porcelain glinting on the shelves, a part of the soft red and blue velvet carpet in which feet sank so pleasantly deep.

The years passed and in the boy's imagination, the room took on huge and mysterious proportions, it was fairy-like in its mysterious enchantment, faraway, unattainable.

And every morning Relly would emerge from therein, with her broom and duster; she would lock the door behind her and heave a deep sigh: 'At least let me keep this room clean!'

On 16 May 1944, two gendarmes with cockerel feathers in their caps, armed with heavy carbines and cartridge belts, entered the Dreispan family home, wearing their big boots, polished in regulation fashion, heedless of the slippers by the front door.

Relly Dreispan, small and thin, with her hair tied in a tall bun on the top of her head; Daniel, her taciturn, mountainous husband; and Roni, their son, who had recently reached the age of nineteen and who had passed his baccalaureate with exceptional marks, were taken from their spotlessly clean house and loaded onto cattle trucks with planks and barbed wire nailed over the ventilation windows.

Each of the forty-three cattle trucks carried seventy souls and a bucket of water, which is to say, three thousand and ten souls in all.

The train set in motion, its metal creaking.

Those within did not know the train's destination.

They had never heard of Auschwitz.

# The Vesuvio Division

From outside in the night came the whistling and laboured puffing of a locomotive. The black outlines of tarpaulin-shrouded cannons and armoured cars loaded on platforms passed before the window of the compartment.

'*Questa e la divisione Vesuvio, che e tutta motorizzata,*' said Vittorio proudly.

'Please, Vittorio, I beg you, don't tell me what division it is or that it's completely motorised… I'm not interested in how many soldiers and officers it has, or how many armoured cars and cannons, or what calibre they are. Please, Vittorio!' said Arnold Josifovitch.

On every fence in town were pasted lugubrious posters: against a black background, a mysterious green face with large, dark, menacing eyes, with a skeletal finger held to its lips. '*Psst! Feind hört mit!*' yelled the posters in jagged red letters like lightning bolts. 'Shush! The enemy is listening!'

The Italian soldiers didn't care about the posters. But that made Arnold Josifovitch all the more anxious.

'Don't tell me what division it is! I don't want to know,' he implored Vittorio.

Tulip Pharmacy said the sign above the door, with a painting of a red tulip, and as Arnold would wrap up soap or cologne, the Italian officer, Captain Luigi Negro, would gravely say, without looking right or left, '*La divisione Vesuvio* is a gift from Il Duce d'Italia to Chancellor Adolf Hitler… He sends us to the Eastern Front against Russia. But what quarrel do we have with the Russians? What have they done to us?'

Captain Luigi Negro, was a short, stocky man with the round olive-skinned face of a man of the south and the hooked nose of a Jewish caricature from *Der Stürmer*. He was a reservist, a teacher from a small town near Naples, and he was very annoyed that he had been taken away from his fourth-year primary school class and brought here to command a battalion of the proud Vesuvio Division, which was completely motorised. And he impotently vented his feeling of misfortune, without looking left or right, and without cautiously lowering his voice. In his despair, which had become chronic and persistent, he no longer cared. Arnold Josifovitch would therefore look right and left all the more. He was afraid he might see somebody listening, silently, wordlessly, to what the Italian said. '*Psst! Feind hört mit!*' He himself might very well be taken for the eavesdropping enemy. Why didn't the captain think of that? Was that the way they talked back in Italy?

Soldiers from three armies were crammed together like sardines in the town of Sighet, in the foothills of the Maramureş Carpathians. Hungarian troops had replaced the Romanian 5th and 9th Alpine Regiments, after the strange, Solomon-like decision to cut the baby in two that had come from Vienna in August 1940, which is to say, the decision to divide Transylvania into two equal parts, generously to be shared between Germany's two smaller allies. The southern part remained in the Kingdom of Romania, and the northern part was ceded to the Kingdom of Hungary, a kingdom without a king, ruled by an admiral without a sea. The Hungarian troops, in their green uniforms, were therefore quartered in the former barracks of the Romanian Alpine Regiments at the edge of town. The German troops, in their dark grey-green uniforms, were quartered in the Palace of Culture and a few schools. It was the summer of the second year of the war, 1942, and the children were on holiday. And the soldiers of the Italian division, in their light grey-green uniforms, similar to those of their German allies, who had been passing through the town, but ended up staying there for a few months, had to make do with being quartered in long trains drawn up on sidings in the town station and in a few rooms requisitioned for the officers in small hotels near the station.

The Hungarian soldiers talked only among themselves. The German soldiers did not talk much even among themselves. The Italian soldiers talked with all and sundry. And they said whatever entered their heads. When they went to buy apples or plums at the market, they talked to the stallholders, in shops they talked to the shopkeepers, they talked to passers-by strolling on the 'Corso', they talked to the barbers and ogled the manicurists, they talked to the waiters in restaurants and public houses. The whole town was filled with the melodious sounds of the Italian language, with strains of the guitar and the mandolin. The Italian soldiers strolled around town casually, without belts and bandoliers, with the top buttons of their tunics undone, or even with two or three buttons open, elegantly nonchalant, and with their military caps rakishly cocked askew; you never saw them with a gun, either a carbine or a holstered service revolver. On the other hand, many carried mandolins and guitars hanging from their thin tunic cross straps or coloured ribbons around their necks; at the very least, they would have a small harmonica in the pocket of their tunics.

And in the evening, from gardens and courtyards, from Mill Park and the silky grass of the banks of the Tisza and Iza, Italian melodies and Neapolitan songs wafted through the town; snatches of *'Mamma son tanto felice, perche ritorno da te'* and *'Non a senso per me, la mia vita senza te'* and *'Sul mare lucido, l'astro d'argento …'* And the whole town hummed along, the young men and women walking in the parks, the housewives doing their shopping and the servant girls following along behind them with the baskets and bags, the market traders, the beggars, the manicurists and the barbers as they shaved and trimmed their customers, the waiters in the restaurants, and even the church and synagogue cantors, who unwittingly incorporated Italian variations and trills in their liturgical chants.

In the middle of the night, languorous serenades gently floated up beneath maidens' windows, like soft white clouds. Lucia Anghel, the daughter of the butter and cheese manufacturer, who lived on Robinia Street, was awoken after midnight, during a full moon, by three young men from '*la divisione Vesuvio*,' one of them singing while the other two accompanied him on guitar and mandolin: '*Amor, amor, amo-o-or… wonderful dream, waking dream… di speranza-a-a…*' And the other two sang in harmony, one high, the other low, '*di speranza-a-a…*' lightly brushing the strings of their mandolin and guitar.

And the three young men did not depart from beneath her window until the girl appeared in the dark window frame holding a flickering candle, her nightdress fluttering around her slender body, a white, angelic apparition.


'Vittorio, please, I beg you, don't tell me what division it is, or that it's completely motorised, or how many cannons and armoured cars it has! I don't want to know military secrets of any kind!' implored Arnold Josifovitch.

Every wall and fence in town was plastered with those black posters with the green face and bloodshot eyes, with the skeletal finger raised to its lips, beneath which it said, '*Psst! Feind hört mit!*' The enemy is listening!

Vittorio looked at him with slight irony. Military secrets? Was he serious? When every mother and sister and wife of the soldiers from the proud '*la divisione Vesuvio*' had sobbed into their handkerchiefs as the train slowly pulled out of the station, and the grandfathers had given quasi-military salutes, holding their hands to their hats and remembering Doberdo and Piave during the Great War. And everybody had been able to count the cannons and armoured cars beneath their thick green tarpaulin on the open platform cars, which snaked behind the passenger carriages packed with soldiers and officers.

The two of them, Arnold Josifovitch and Vittorio Morandi, were sitting in a compartment of a passenger carriage. As a matter of fact, Arnold was the guest of Vittorio, whom he had met when he came into his father's pharmacy. Arnold helped his father behind the counter and Vittorio had come in to buy soap and toothpaste. A few times, on Sundays, when the pharmacy was closed, Vittorio had visited him at home. When the tall Italian, his chestnut hair cropped short and standing up like the bristles of a hedgehog, had first come to their house, Arnold's mother, Mrs Roza Josifovitch, had taken fright. What was a soldier doing in her house? She didn't know what kind of soldier he was or what he wanted. But his father, Mr David Josifovitch, who had by now also met him at the pharmacy, where he took turns with his son behind the counter, reassured her. 'He's a very nice Italian, very friendly.' Although he himself didn't find his son's friendship with a soldier of Mussolini particularly reassuring. But Vittorio entered their house unselfconsciously, as if he had been their son's friend since childhood: 'Is Arnoldo at home?' And the young Vittorio and Arnold, and his younger sister, who was seventeen, talked among themselves in a mixture of Italian and Romanian, or Romanian and Italian, aided by sign language and words in Hungarian and German, and they understood each other wonderfully. And they drank a little liqueur and ate homemade *gerbeaud* cake, and they joked and they laughed. What was so frightening about that? And besides, never before had they told any friend of Arnold not to come to their house.

Once, Vittorio told him, 'Arnoldo' – that was what he called him, with an Italian 'o' at the end – 'I've been to your house many times, why don't you come and see where I live?'

Such an invitation one cannot decline.

And so one evening, Vittorio took him to the station, they crossed the railway tracks and arrived at a series of dark sidings, where rows of trains were standing.

Somebody asked him something and Vittorio answered, maybe a password, or quite simply a word to recognise him by, and they entered one of the carriages.

'This is *casa mia*,' said Vittorio, rather sourly.

It was a second-class compartment with two pairs of bunk beds, dimly lit by a bulb in the ceiling. They sat down facing each other on the lower of the two bunk beds. Vittorio produced a bottle of sweet Tuscan wine and two small loaves of white bread, baked without salt to make them keep fresh for longer.

They sipped wine and nibbled the insipid white bread.

Outside, through the window, the lights of the station could be seen twinkling in the distance through the murk. Here and there swung the red lanterns of the points men. From time to time the whistle and chug of a manoeuvring locomotive could be heard. At intervals, long platform cars passed by the window, with the black shapes of cannons and armoured cars.

'Don't worry, I'm not going to tell you anything about the division's brand-new cannons,' laughed Vittorio.

All of a sudden, his other three bunkmates burst into the compartment: Carlo Bottini and two other soldiers of the Vesuvio division, one of them with a guitar, the other with a mandolin hanging from his bandolier.

'The Milanese are here! Bravo!' exclaimed Vittorio, sarcastically.

'Well, if you insist on making savings,' replied Carlo, a chubby young man with a round face and short black hair glistening with brilliantine.

The three newcomers were not at all surprised at Arnold being there in the compartment.

'You know, Tuscans like to talk a lot. They work hard, too, no denying that, but they're niggardly, they squirrel away all their money and walk around wearing threadbare trousers,' said Carlo to Arnold.

'And Milanese talk little, they're hardworking, no denying that, but they spend all their money on clothes. If you picked up a Milanese by his crisply pressed trousers and shook him, nothing but pumpkin seeds would fall out of his pockets.'

'Better that than having scruffy, un-ironed trousers!' chipped in Bernardo Coccino, a short, swarthy lad.

'What are you butting in for? You're the crossbreed of a Milano man and a Sicilian from Syracuse, and you sing requests for Neapolitan ditties…'

The third newcomer, Antonio Reni, a ginger-haired, freckled lad, began twanging his guitar, singing, *'Amor, amor, amo-o-or… Wonderful dream, all the girls bedded with Bottini Carlo-o-o…'*

Carlo's round face turned as red as a beetroot.

'Shut up, Antonio! Don't be a boor! I love her… very much… *Io la voglio bene, molto bene…'*

They all fell silent for a few moments.

'Where are your glasses?' Vittorio suddenly said. And he poured each one a glass of Tuscan wine.

That was the way the men of the Vesuvio division teased each other, the soldiers sent by Il Duce Mussolini to the Eastern Front.

From outside there came a series of long blasts on a bugle.

'What's that?' asked Arnold.

'Lights out! All the nice, well-behaved children have to say their prayers and go to bed now.'

'Then I'd better be going.'

'But we're not nice, well-behaved children,' said Vittorio.

And they all burst out laughing.

The light in the compartment went out. Straight away the soldiers lit candles. They chatted, laughed and joked, sipped wine and nibbled the unsalted military bread until after midnight.

Vittorio conducted Arnold to the edge of the station's military zone, after which Arnold made his way down the deserted streets of the town, which were dimly lit by anaemic bulbs atop tall wooden poles, and finally arrived home.

He had to pass his parents' bedroom to reach his own room. Arnold took off his shoes lest he make a sound, but his mother hadn't been able to fall sleep for worry.

'What time is it, Arnie?' came her voice from the darkened room.

In fright, Arnold stopped in his tracks.

'It's ten, Mama.'

To his misfortune, in the dining room the old clock with the brass pendulum struck one at just that moment.

'Did you hear that? It struck one, Arnie!' said his mother reproachfully.

'What do you expect, Mama, for it to strike the zero too?' said Arnold, annoyed, and quickly went to bed in his own room.


A few days later, Vittorio burst into the Josifovitchs' chemist's shop, the charmingly named Tulip Pharmacy, almost choking with indignation. It was as if his cropped head bristled more spikily.

'Do you know what I saw, Arnoldo? Something unbelievable! I was passing the Hungarians' barracks and there in the yard I saw an officer yelling at the soldier polishing his boots. And then he struck him across the face with a riding crop.'

'It was his orderly. Don't your officers have orderlies?'

'Yes, we do, but only if the soldier agrees to be an orderly. He can't be forced to. And if he agrees, the officer has to pay him like any other worker. For a while, I was Captain Luigi Negro's orderly. But then I didn't want to be any more, so I gave it up. But for somebody to have raised his hand to me and struck me with a riding crop… Unimaginable! I would have snatched the riding crop from his hand and, officer or no, I would have given him a good thrashing with it.'

'And you would have been court martialled!'

'Maybe in your army I would have. But not in our army. An officer isn't allowed to raise his hand to his orderly, and the orderly isn't obliged to polish the officer's boots when he's still wearing them, but only after he's taken them off. And if the officer doesn't like the job his orderly does, then let him find a different one.'

All of a sudden, Vittorio fell silent. A Hungarian officer entered the pharmacy, wearing a crisp green uniform with red epaulettes and holding a silver-handled riding crop tucked under his arm. A lieutenant in the Hungarian Army.

'What can we do for you, lieutenant, sir?'

He asked for cologne. On the counter, Arnold placed before him a range of bottles, large and small, of various brands. The officer wrinkled his nose in dissatisfaction. There were now fifteen bottles, vials and flacons on the counter. The handsome officer, with his gleaming black hair and grey eyes, regarded them scornfully. 'What tastes, *Istenem!*' he murmured. Finally, he decided and pointed vaguely at one of the bottles.

'How much?'

'One *pengő* and thirty *fillér*,' replied Arnold.

The officer paid the sum. Arnold wrapped the bottle nicely and handed it to him.

'Here are you are. Thank you!'

The officer looked at him in indignation.

'What do you take me for? Do you expect me to put it in my pocket? Have it delivered to me at home!'

And he gave him his visiting card. It had a seven-pointed crown and was inscribed thus:

Vitéz Baró Hottinfalvi Hottiny Károly
M. Kir. Honvédfőhadnagy
75. Honvéd Ezred

Arnold himself was indignant. A small bottle costing one *pengő* and a few *fillér* and he wants to have it delivered to him! But he said politely, 'As you wish, lieutenant, sir!'

'Did you not read my visiting card?' said the officer-baron, indignant anew.

'My apologies, *Méltóságos Uram*, Your Excellency!' Arnold quickly corrected himself.

The officer stalked out of the pharmacy muttering to himself, 'Such ill-bred, ill-mannered people here in Erdély!'[1]

After the officer left, Arnold said, 'I shouldn't wonder if that was the very officer who yelled at his orderly and struck him with his riding crop.'

'No, it wasn't,' he answered, with a meaningful wink. 'But he looked a lot like him, he was just as proud and haughty, held his head just as stiffly, and had a silver-handled riding crop just like his. And probably he's just as valiant in front of his own orderly...'

And they both burst out laughing.

In the town of Sighet, opposite the station, there was a small hotel and restaurant, a long, single-storey building whose dirty-grey façade formed the background for crooked green letters that read 'Hotel Zona Szálloda'. The business was run by the Tatzenhaus family. In fact, 'run by the family' is not entirely accurate, since the hotel, with its eight rooms along the length of a narrow corridor and its restaurant dining room at the front, with its old tables and chairs and its counter with a drawer for the takings, was in fact run by Mrs Tatzenhaus. She was the only one who put money in that cash drawer; the others only took money out of it. Her husband, Mekil, was a short, red-headed man as hot as pepper, who liked to rush around all day long in pursuit of business opportunities that never bore fruit. He did his rushing mostly in a cab, urging the driver to make the nag go faster, so much

---

1 Erdély: Hungarian name for Transylvania – *Translator's note*

so that when folk asked him once why he was standing rather than sitting in the hurtling cab, Mekil answered, 'Because I'm in a hurry.' He liked to rush around on business that involved brokering marriages and the sale of houses; buying and selling bargains: Singer sewing machines and Underwood typewriters with small defects; joining 'associations' of traders in herring and fatted geese. But above all, Mekil liked to play cards in the evening in the lounges at the back of the Corona Café in the centre of town, and for that he needed money, which he secretly removed from the cash drawer. Their son, Simion Tatzenhaus, also secretly took money from the long-suffering drawer, because he liked to spend his nights at Le Jardin, a different kind of restaurant, and more often than not the drawer paid for the lengthy medical treatment he subsequently had to undergo, treatment that the venereal diseases specialist sometimes lengthened even further, given its profitability, and which had to remain hidden from his parents. Their twin daughters, Mara and Clara, with their curly red hair, also took money from the drawer, when they felt the need to buy perfumes or lotions or anti-freckle creams.

The only member of the family who stood at the counter and put money in the drawer was Mrs Serena Tatzenhaus. When the Hungarians took over northern Transylvania, Serena was radiant with joy. She remembered the good times, during the reign of Ferencz-Jóska, as they used to nickname Franz-Josef I, Emperor of Austria-Hungary, King of Bohemia, Moravia, Serbia, Bosnia and Herzegovina, and so on, and so on. But she soon realised that these were not the same Hungarians. When the horse-riding admiral, the Regent of Hungary, whose white horse had been conveyed to Baia-Mare by special train, and who himself arrived in a luxury carriage, with an upholstered couch and armchairs, arrived at the edge of Baia-Mare, *vitéz nagybányai* Horthy Miklós mounted his white horse and haughtily proceeded to the rat-a-tat of drums and the blare of trumpets, Mrs Serena Tatzenhaus, who was avidly reading about the event in the newspaper and who had a sense of humour, couldn't help but laugh at that bombastic entrance and began to realise that whatever else he might have been, the Emperor Franz-Josef was a far more serious man.

Later, when the 'Jewish laws' arrived one hot on the heels of the other, and she had to surrender the hotel, restaurant, cash drawer and all, when the whole family had to vacate the house where they lived and move into a single cramped room on Tanners Street, in the ghetto, when the gendarmes with black cockerel feathers in their caps drove them out of that room, marched them to the ramp of Sighet station and loaded them onto cattle trucks whose ventilation windows had been nailed shut with planks and barbed wire, Mrs Serena Tatzenhaus perfectly realised that they were not at all the same Hungarians as they had been in the wonderful days of Ferencz-Jóska.

But in 1942, when the Hungarians entered Sighet and the Italians of the Vesuvio division were still there in transit, things still going quite well, or even very well: the Zona Restaurant was full and the soldiers of three nations came there to drink beer and pinch the waitresses.

There was particular merriment after the Italians arrived in the restaurant dining room. The tables were almost permanently occupied; there was drinking, loud talking, joking, laughing, teasing between tables. The Italians also invited their fresh acquaintances to join them, girls and boys from the town.

One Sunday evening, in the noisy, crowded restaurant dining room, at a number of tables joined together, there sat Vittorio Morandi, the hardworking, thrifty young mechanic from Volterra in the Tuscany region; Carlo Bottini, the son of a wealthy vermouth exporter from Milan; the short and swarthy Bernardo Coccino, the crossbreed of a Milanese father and a Sicilian mother from Syracuse; the freckled Antonio Reni; Mauro Guadrini, Mario de Carlo, Giovanni Bianchi, Amadeo Baccarini, and other lads from 'la divisione'; Arnold Josifovitch, who worked for his father at the Tulip

Pharmacy; Simion Tatzenhaus, a ginger-haired lad with a hooked nose like his father's, the son of Mrs Serena, the guardian of the drawer from which the whole family pilfered; and a number of their friends from when they were at school, such as Gustav Knochl, an Austrian whose father had been a lieutenant in the army of the Emperor Franz-Josef; Miron Hotea, the son of the public notary from the village of Bocicoiu, and Tibi Sárai, the son of a journalist, who dreamed of becoming a doctor and always went around with a small briefcase in which he kept a large syringe and a bottle of potassium permanganate; and other young men whom the Italians had insisted come and sit at their table. They were drinking Maramureş plum brandy and Martini and Cinzano: some drank from stemmed glasses, some from beer mugs, depending on each drinker's inclination, and they were also munching crusty rolls sprinkled with salt and caraway seeds. Simion Tatzenhaus was cracking jokes about the Negus of Abyssinia, some of them rather inane, jokes that were unfamiliar to the Italians, but which had been very popular a few years before, when the Duce was waging war against Haile Selassie. The jokes were harmless enough, they insulted nobody, neither the Negus nor Mussolini, but their purpose – for everything in the world has a purpose – seemed to be simply to keep alive the memory of the past. Who knows? Maybe their purpose was sheer playfulness, to keep the mind sharp, albeit with a blunt knife?

'Why does the Negus wear red braces?' asked Simion.

Naturally, none of the Italians knew. It was the first they'd heard about the Negus wearing red braces.

'So that his trousers won't fall down.'

They all burst out laughing.

'What is it when the Negus spits in the snow?'

Amazement. Snow, in Abyssinia?

'It's winter!'

The Italians laughed to split their sides, and their local friends laughed too, carried away by their merriment.

All of a sudden two German soldiers entered the restaurant.

'Heil Hitler!' they barked in unison.

They were exactly the same height, their uniforms were identically tidy, well-brushed, buttoned to the neck, regulation fashion, they each wore steel helmets and diagonal belts for the holsters of their automatics, and their two pairs of black jackboots shone with equal lustre.

Silence abruptly fell, as if the noise had been lopped off with a whetted razor. Everybody looked down and studied his own glass, although each was perfectly familiar with its contents.

The two German soldiers approached the counter, each in perfect step, and made their order.

'Bier, bitte!'

'Bier, bitte!'

Mrs Serena served them personally.

There was perfect silence in the dining room. Not a sound. Not even the buzzing of a fly, although there were plenty of flies that summer. Not even the creak of a chair, although there were plenty of chairs that creaked.

The Germans thirstily drank their beer. Each then exhaled in satisfaction. Each placed his mug on the counter at the same time.

'No, ja!' said the one.

'No, ja!' agreed the other.

They then took another few swigs.

'Gut!' said the one.

'Gut!' agreed the other.

They drank once more. They both reached the bottom of their mugs at the same time.

Making the same gestures, each counted out thirty *filler* onto the counter, which Mrs Serena swept into the drawer.

They made a regulation salute, crying 'Heil Hitler!' and marched heavily back out, in perfect step.

After a few moments, Vittorio quietly said, *'Si, si! I Tedeschi sono soldati, cento per cento!'*

Yes, yes, the Germans were soldiers one hundred per cent, agreed the others, nodding mutely.

Noise and merriment returned to the restaurant dining room, the clink of glasses and the munching of crusty rolls, the conversation that rose above the tables, the swarming flies that buzzed all summer long, and the creaking of chairs, as if they had never been interrupted.

'Tell me, what's the difference between a seventeen-year-old Abyssinian girl and a nineteen-year-old Italian girl?' asked Simion.

The answer? 'Two years!'

They all laughed. And they drank their glasses of Maramureş plum brandy, Martini, Cinzano, and their mugs of beer, each to his own fancy.

'Carlo, what's up with you?' Vittorio suddenly asked. 'You've been completely absent all evening.'

'No, I haven't!' objected Carlo.

But Vittorio was right. Carlo Bottini had been completely absent all evening. His mind was elsewhere.


Vittorio Morandi was a young man full of curiosity, who went through life wide-eyed, curious to see, hear, discover new things.

One Saturday afternoon, he turned up at the Josifovitch family home unexpectedly. The father was reading from the *Pirkei Avot*, the *Teachings of the Fathers*, and Roza and the children, Arnold and Elisabeth, were listening attentively or distractedly, according to the mood of each; it was a tradition to read a chapter from this book of the Talmud and Mr David Josifovitch cherished it. All week long he sold bars of soap, bottles of perfume, and various creams, and it made him feel good to take on the rôle of teacher at the end of the week ... 'The same Hillel once saw the head of a drowned man floating at the surface of the water and he said: Because you drowned another, they drowned you, and he who drowned you will also be drowned.' And in satisfaction, smoothing his chestnut beard, the paterfamilias set about explaining that good is rewarded with good, and evil is punished with evil, and Elisabeth, his daughter, interrupted, 'Father, you've explained it to us countless times, and it isn't quite like that, but read on,' and Roza, her mother, cast her a scolding look when all of a sudden Vittorio Morandi appeared in the doorway, out of breath – it was plain that he had been running – and called out in fear and amazement: 'Do you know what I saw, Arnoldo?'

'What did you see?'

'A *giudeo*!'

'You don't say, Vittorio! Are you sure?' replied Arnold, ironically. All of them looked at him in fear and bewilderment.

'Yes, yes,' said Vittorio. 'I saw him with my own eyes, he had a big round black hat, as big as a tray, and a long beard, and curly hair like two tubes here, in front of his ears. And he had a big hooked nose. And the Germans told us that they were bad men, parasites, traders and usurers, who steal and cheat and suck the blood of the people.'

For a few minutes, a deep silence settled over the house. Mrs Roza looked at her husband, frightened, mute, as if to say, 'I told you so!' But Arnold recovered his wits and said, 'Vittorio, we're *giudei* too, we're Jews…'

'Impossible! What are you saying, Arnoldo?' blurted the Italian, in confusion.

'Yes, yes! I'm a Jew. Father is a Jew, look at his beard, like Pirandello's, even if he doesn't have the curly hair in front of his ears, he's a Jew. And Mother is a Jew, my sister Elisabeta is a Jew. And Simion Tatzenhaus is a *giudeo*, and his mother, Mrs Serena, is a Jew, and his sisters, Clara and Mara, are Jews, and his father is a Jew, a red-headed one like Antonio Reni, without a beard, but with a big hooked nose, which is just like Captain Luigi Negro's, who is an Italian, a Neapolitan born and bred… Aren't there lots of Catholics too, Vittorio, who wear black hats as big as trays and long black coats like caftans? And aren't there monks with shaved heads, who wear brown habits made of sackcloth tied with a rope at the waist?'

Arnold fell silent for a few moments, then went on.

'I studied at the economics high-school and I learned that it was the Lombards who were the great bankers and usurers of the modern world, but nobody said they "suck the blood of the people". And it was said, half in jest, half seriously, that in the hierarchy of merchants, the Jewish people hold third place, that a Greek merchant is worth two Arabs, that an Arab merchant is worth three Jews… And as is well known, among the Germans, commerce is held in high esteem… as long as it's conducted by Germans. And lately in particular, it hasn't been conducted by Jews…'

Silence. Arnold's voice grew fainter and fainter, wearier and wearier.

'And besides, for God's sake, Vittorio, we're not a uniform mass of merchants and usurers, some of us are tradesmen, tailors, cobblers, carpenters, locksmiths, photographers, bakers, cake makers, and all kinds of other occupations, and not all of us are filthy rich, some of us are poor, unfortunately…'

Vittorio, the young mechanic from Tuscany, listened, glowering, like a man deceived for the umpteenth time, a man lied to for the umpteenth time in his short life.

He remained silent for a time, embarrassed, and then mumbled, 'I didn't know, Arnoldo. I've never seen a *giudeo*, or maybe I have, but without knowing he was…'

And from that afternoon hence, they never spoke of it again.

The mother maintained her frightened silence from the moment Vittorio uttered the word *giudeo* in her house. Nor did the daughter, Elisabeth, say another word, and the father, with his Pirandello goatee, remained silent, too. But now he continued to read from the *Teachings of the Fathers*, in a soft voice.

'The wise man Hillel said: If I am not for myself, who will be for me? And if I am only for myself, what am I? And if not now, then when? And the great Shkhamai said: "Set a time for thyself in which to study, speak little and do much. And welcome each man with a smile on thy face."

Vittorio listened attentively, along with the others.

Captain Luigi Negro – it was pronounced 'Nero,' with the *g* almost completely swallowed by the following *r* – was depressed. He missed his wife and four children, whom he had left behind in Torre-Anunciata, his small town near Naples. And he missed all the children he had taught to the end of their fourth year and whom now he ought to have been teaching in their fifth year. But he had had to take command of an armoured unit of the Vesuvio division, which was completely motorised; he had had to depart for the east, passing through Sighet on the way, a town he had never heard of, and would never have heard of back home in Torre Anunciata.

Captain Negro was depressed, disconsolate. All the more so since it was almost his birthday, which fell on 23 August, the last day of the zodiac sign, Leo. He was about to reach the age of forty, and for the first time in his life he would be spending his birthday far away from his family, all alone, staring into a glass of red wine as he sat in a train carriage on a railway siding. Or so he imagined.

But he didn't spend his birthday on his own. On finding out the date of his birthday, a few of the soldiers in his unit secretly organised a celebratory meal.

Behind the Zona Hotel and Restaurant there was a little garden with sparse grass and a few plum trees. The young men carried the ping-pong table from the yard into the garden and joined to it another couple of tables from the restaurant. It was evening, and on the table burned dozens of candles, bottles of wine and vermouth glinted, there were trays laden with cubes of hard and soft cheese, sliced tomatoes and green peppers, and loaves of white Italian military bread, baked without salt so that it wouldn't go mouldy or stale too quickly. And in the middle of the table there was a cake with white icing, made by Mrs Serena Tatzenhaus, a tall cake in the shape of a tower, on which burned four thick candles.

Around these large tables, on benches and chairs brought from the restaurant and from the Tatzenhaus family home, the soldiers took their places: the short, swarthy Bernardo Coccino, son of a Lombardian father and a Sicilian mother, who sang Neapolitan songs on his mandolin, and the freckled, red-headed Antonio Reni, with his guitar resting on the seat next to him, and Mauro Guardini, who worked in the Il Vesuvio bakery of his father in Reggio di Calabria and was preparing to study the engineering of bakery machinery in Rome, to fulfil his father's dream, and Giovanni Bianchi, and Mario de Carlo, and others from the unit; also taking their place at the table were young people from the town: Simion Tatzenhaus, the son of Mrs Serena, who guarded, without success, the cash drawer of the Zona Hotel and Restaurant, and Arnold Josifovitch, who had finished economics school and wanted to become a diplomat or a commercial attaché at the very least, but who in the meantime helped out his father in the Tulip Pharmacy. Also at the table was Ebi Friedberg, whose widowed mother owned a flour mill, and Marcu Marcovitch-Dox, thus nicknamed because he had avidly read every comic in the series *The Adventures of Submarine Dox* and *The Adventures of the Dox Crew* and who wanted to become the captain of a merchant ship, to roam the waves, to dock in exotic, sun-kissed tropical ports, and Gustav Knochl, an alumnus of the economics school, originally from Vienna, whose father had been a lieutenant in the army of Emperor Franz-Josef. They had tried to persuade Gustav to join the Volksbund, an organisation for ethnic Germans, but he had stubbornly refused, because *Leutenant* Knochl, his father, had given his children a barracks education, forbidding them 'to get mixed up in politics.' Gustav Knochl's inclinations tended in a completely different direction. He was in love with mechanisms, with nuts, bolts, screws. He collected the nuts, bolts and screws he found on the street, and his ambition was to build a motorcycle from the various parts he discovered lying around or bought when he could afford it. In the shed in his yard, he now had an old pair of handlebars, a pedal, and a spoked motorcycle wheel, without a tyre. Also at the table, seated on a kitchen stool, was Tibi Sárai, the son of a journalist, who was set on being a doctor and in the meantime treated his classmates' gonorrhoea with potassium permanganate, which he injected with the huge syringe he always carried in his satchel along with his textbooks and exercise books. Also present was Miron Hotea, the son of a public notary from Bocicoiu, a strapping young man who was later to cross the Carpathians clandestinely and join the Romanian marines. Around the ping-pong table there were also a few girls: Mara and Clara, the redheaded twins, Simion Tatzenhaus's sisters; Eliza, Arnold Josifovitch's sisters, who were pupils at the Princess Ileana of Romania school, whose name was now the Piarist Gymnasium; and other girls from the town. They were all awaiting the arrival of Captain Negro with great excitement.

Carlo Bottini and Vittorio Morandi went to fetch him and when Captain Negro set eyes on the festive table, on the tall cake shaped like a white bastion on which the candles were twinkling merrily, on the radiant faces of the young folk, he was left speechless for a few moments.

A chorus of voices, accompanied by guitars and mandolins, rang forth: *'Buon compleanno! Tanti Auguri!'* The captain's eyes grew moist; he was unable to say a single word.

They invited him to sit in the tall-backed chair set aside for him at the head of the table.

*'Grazie! Grazie tanto…'* stammered the captain, his voice choking.

They clinked glasses, munched white Italian military bread with hard and soft cheese, slices of tomato and pepper. And the more they clinked, the more the merriment grew.

Carlo Bottini was laughing too loudly. And singing too softly, almost in disgust.

'What's up with you, Carlo?' Vittorio, who was sitting next to him, asked in a whisper. 'Did you invite her?'

'She can't come. Her parents won't let her.'

'A proud division, very proud,' said Luigi Negro in a tender, melancholy voice, '*la divisione Vesuvio*, completely motorised, with four hundred and seventy armoured cars and two hundred cannons, the most modern equipment…'

'He's talking about the division,' thought Arnold bitterly, 'and about the armoured cars and the equipment, when on every fence and wall in the town the posters are screaming, *"Psst! Feind hört mit!"*' But he didn't say anything. Who cared after the seventh glass?

'This is a very nice little town we're staying in here, it's rather like Italian mountain towns,' the captain went on. 'A dream. Who would ever have imagined he'd end up in Sighet, Maramureş, here in the foothills of the Carpathians? But what are we doing here, in fact? Ah, yes, we're in transit, on our way to the Eastern Front. When they sent us to Abyssinia, we knew that we were going to conquer that primitive country for Italy, to lift it up, to civilise it… When they sent us to North Africa to fight alongside General Rommel's troops, they said we were defending Abyssinia and Italy's interests in Africa. When we attacked Greece, a neighbouring country, an old and civilised country, we were amazed, disappointed, bitter, but we told ourselves, it was a question of politics, it was so that it wouldn't fall into the hands of Hitler, since Greece is part of the Mediterranean… And Il Duce wants to revive the glory of Rome, to make the Mediterranean a *Mare Romanum*. A big Roman pond, in other words. So be it! But what are we doing in Russia? It's so far from the Mediterranean… What quarrel do we have with the Russians? They're Bolsheviks! So what? They're Bolsheviks and we're Fascists. But the Russians don't send any motorised armoured divisions to Italy…'

'How does he dare to talk like that?' said Knochl, nudging Simion Tatzenhaus beneath the table.

'What can they do to him? Send him to the Eastern Front?' said Simion, stifling a laugh.

Captain Negro took a sip of wine and went on, 'This time we can be proud. We, the fifteen thousand two hundred and eighty-three soldiers and officers of the Vesuvio division, are a gift! A wonderful gift from Il Duce, which he has paid as a tribute to the Führer and Reichskanzler of Germany, that we might plug a hole in the front for him and conquer a strip of Russian land... And when we go back home, covered in glory, we'll tell the schoolchildren how many ferocious Russians we've slain. And the children will gaze on us in admiration and say, 'What a hero Father is!' And they'll stroke the medals on our chest...'

Schoolteacher Luigi Negro burst into uncontrollable laughter. Nobody laughed with him, and a deep silence suddenly descended over the table, which lasted for a good few minutes.

Then, from somewhere behind the table, there came a muffled, slightly slurring voice, which sang, *'Sul mare lucido l'astro d'argento-o-o...'* It was Bernardo Coccino, who could no longer bear the tense silence. A few others began to accompany him on guitar and mandolin, singing the refrain. It was true, the 'silver star' really was floating in the sky that night, pale and gentle, it shone on the glistening sea by Naples, on the small town of Torre-Anunciata, on the forested mountains of Maramureş, on the town of Sighet, on the table spread in honour of Captain Luigi Negro's birthday. Then, Ebi Friedberg, the son of the widow who owned the flour mill, began to sing in a low voice, in a Jewish C minor, 'Where are my seven good years?' as if somebody had made a firm promise to give him them. But this is what he had heard his grandmother sing when he was still in the cradle: 'Where are my seven good years? And if not seven, then at least three... Something, at least, from this life.' This is what the poor, sorrowful woman had pleaded to the Lord Above. And Tibi Sárai, who was determined to become a doctor and always carried around a huge syringe in his satchel, sang about the gypsy camp in Pecica, where all had gathered around, weeping and moaning for the sovereign of fiddlers, who lay dying on his woollen rug, and the Voivode of the gypsies, on whose face could no longer be read dignity, but only grief, asked him his last wish before he met the Voivode Father in heaven. Should the priest be summoned? No, there was no need of a priest, what good was a priest? He had a single desire: that his violin be laid in the grave beside him. And when he arrived there, up above, before the throne of the Voivode Father, he would play it as only he knew how, that he might mollify Him, that he might soften His heart for the persecuted gypsy race.

And Gusti Knochl, who played some seven musical instruments – at home he played first violin in a string trio with his father and sister – accompanied the songs now on mandolin, now on guitar, now on harmonica, covering up any false notes on the part of the others with great talent. Then he himself solemnly played a number of lieder, lightly plucking the strings of his guitar.

The Italians were astonishingly quick to pick up the tunes, which they were hearing for the first time in their lives, and provided a cautious vocal and instrumental accompaniment.

Miron Hotea, the son of the public notary from Bocicoi, handed Gusti the shepherd's whistle he always carried in the inside pocket of his jacket, along with a fountain pen, and loudly said, 'Repeat each line after me!' And in a melancholy but firm voice, he began:

*Măi, frăţîne, eu şi tu.*

All repeated the line.

*Şohan, n-om videa raiu!*

'Alas, little brother, thou and I. Never will we see heaven!' said Miron, translating the dialect of the Maramureş peasant.

*Da' nici nu-i hie să-l videm!*

'But there is no need for us to see it,' explained Miron.

*După ce feciori sîntem*
*Fii, Raiule, sănătos,*
*Că noi om me' mai pe din jos…*

'Yes, yes, we'll go on foot here on this earth and then down under!' cried a number of those around the table.

Miron Hotea continued to sing, accompanied by Gusti Knochl on shepherd's whistle and Sárai, Josifovitch and others:

> Cîtu-i Maramureşu,
> Cîtu-i Maramureşu,
> Nu-i fecior ca eu şi tu,
> Nici oraş ca Sighetu.

'Si, si! Non ce una cittá come Sighet!' repeated the Italians.

Miron went on, satisfied that they had picked up the tune:

> Şi cite flori pe Iza în sus,
> Toate cu mîndra le-am pus.
> Şi cite le-am pus pînă-n prînz,
> Toate-s mîndre şi s-au prins.
> Şi cite le-am pus pînă-n cină,
> S-au uscat din rădăcină.

Sárai Tibi, who dreamed of becoming a doctor, took up the droning, monotonous tune and sang his favourite poem, while the others hummed along:

> Săraca inima mea,
> Sireaca inima mea,
> M-am dus la doctor cu ea,
> La doctor şi la potica,
> Dar n-am hăznuit nimică,
> Poticarăşul mi-a spus,
> Leacuri la inimă nu-s.
> La inimă este un leac:
> Cetera şi omul drag.

Vittorio and Carlo, for whom Arnold translated the words as best he could, cried out in enthusiasm, raising their glasses: 'Si, si! I violin e l'uomo caro!'

And so it was that at the feast to celebrate Captain Luigi Negro's birthday, they drank wine and beer and Italian vermouth, and they ate cubes of soft and hard cheese and slices of tomato and green pepper, and together they sang Italian, Neapolitan, Hungarian, Gypsy, Romanian and Jewish songs, songs that were not at war with each other, but coexisted in peace and harmony.

And they made merry until the pale white light of dawn began to show in the sky.

A sensational rumour began to circulate in Sighet. One of the local girls had secretly got engaged to an Italian. From him she had even received a platinum ring with a large diamond. And after the war, when he returned from the Eastern Front, he was going to fetch her and take her back to Italy with him. Nobody knew which girl had got engaged or to which Italian. It was even said that the ring wasn't really platinum, nor was the diamond genuine. But the rumour of the engagement persisted.

All day long, the din of the town, the hubbub of the streets, the haggling and quarrelling in the food markets and the hay and cattle marts, the rattling of the little factories that made candles and bars of soap and brushes and butter and cheeses, the clanking of the looms that wove *tallits* – prayer shawls – and tablecloths, mingled with snatches of melodies floating in the air. Italian soldiers in their grey-green uniforms, with the top buttons undone, despite regulations, roamed the streets with guitars and mandolins hanging from the bandoliers.

And in the evening, when the din gradually died away, the sound of the songs became clearer; the town was rocked by gentle melodies and languorous serenades that rose beneath the windows of girls from good families.

And couples strolled in the parks, and they sat on benches or on the tender grass on the banks of the Tisza and Iza, the rivers that girdled the town, making it almost an island, or they climbed the winding paths up to the top of Solovan Hill. And there were silences and promises: 'We shall return and then …'

Very late, long after the serenades were over, on moonless nights the young people headed to the Le Jardin Café-Bar at the edge of town, in a quarter exotically called *Bandjalgo*, although nobody knew why. Despite the name, there was no garden, but only a long, shabby-looking one-storey building, behind which there was an inner courtyard surrounded by squat buildings, each of whose rooms had its own door and window. You could reach this courtyard via a portal or through the saloon of the café-bar.

Although it was called a café-bar, in the saloon, with its red sofas along the walls and its little tables in the corners, brandy and vermouth was served more often than coffee. Heavily made-up and perfumed girls, with two-syllable feline names like Mitzi, Fritzi, Pitzi, Tantzi and Molly, sat on the drapes over the worn red velvet of the sofas, striking provocative, enticing positions. At an old piano, a thin man in a threadbare frock coat played old ballads, alternating them with jaunty foxtrots and languorous tangos. And there was always a *Damenwahl* there. After an exchange of glances, the girls would invite one or another of the customers to dance and then, putting on a spoiled air, in nasal tones they would invite their dance partner to order some vermouth or cognac or champagne or the 'gentleman's favourite drink.' The more the customer drank or the more expensive the beverage, the higher the girl's prestige and the stronger her position among the others.

From time to time, a customer would vanish with one of the perfumed, garishly made-up girls, and after a while he would slip back into the saloon unnoticed.

'Didn't you go out with Mitzi?' Arnold asked his friend. Mitzi was the favourite of Ebi Friedberg, the son of the widow who owned the flour mill.

'Yes, I did, but I'm back!' replied Friedberg angrily. He was short, stocky, and when he was angry he seemed even shorter, and his nose, raised in the air, seemed even pointier.

'What happened?' asked Arnold, discreetly.

'She read the newspaper. Can you imagine? There I was on top of her, doing my utmost, panting and sweating, and with her right hand, she took the newspaper from the bedside table and holding it above my head, she started reading it in the glow from the red lampshade. Can you imagine? Now that the Italians are here and they're all queuing at Mitzi's door, the glory has gone to her head. But just you wait till they've left… She'll be desperate to see me then, but she'll have to wait long and hard…'

Unlike in the other cafés and restaurants of Sighet, the Le Jardin saloon wasn't noisy, and the customers spoke quietly, discreetly, it was as if a sinful silence hung on the air.

That night, Carlo Bottini, the son of the rich vermouth merchant from Milan, was singing, accompanied by Bernardo Coccino on guitar and Antonio Reni on mandolin, and by a few other friends, who sang harmony or played harmonicas in between drinking glass after glass of imported Cinzano. Molly, the youngest and most beautiful of the girls, had latched onto him and wouldn't let him go. Molly had dusky skin, a narrow waist, full hips, long, almost sculpted legs, and breasts that jiggled beneath her brassiere. She did not allow just anybody to caress them. Only special customers, who paid a special fee, could touch their roundness. Molly was very much in demand and could have retired to her room in the courtyard many times, but she had latched onto the young, slightly chubby Lombard with the round, girl-like face and naïve smile… Yes, probably it was Carlo's pure, serene smile that attracted her. '*Bello mio*,' she teased him; *'caro mio,'* she called the young Milanese and kissed his flushed, round face, and stroked his slick black hair, which glistened with brilliantine. His melancholy song went straight to the girl's heart. She pulled him toward the middle of the room and he danced, hugging her tightly, as if floating over the parquet, his eyes closed, enraptured. When the dance ended, she drew him after her, toward her room, but he suddenly awoke from his euphoria and stood rooted to the spot. He couldn't be budged; it was as if the soles of his feet were glued to the parquet.

The whole night, Carlo Bottini drank with Molly, he danced with her, transported, but he would not let himself be taken to her room.

At dawn, after the lads had left, Molly found three large, rumpled banknotes in her imitation snakeskin handbag.

In autumn 1942, when the order came that within three days the motorised Vesuvio division was to proceed to the Eastern Front, for three days and nights the guitars and mandolins and harmonicas played the same Neapolitan and Italian canzonets, but how sad they now sounded.

And on the third day, in the month of September, the trains moved out of the station, at short intervals, one after the other. The locomotives puffed, the wheels clacked rhythmically, and the soldiers looked out of the windows of the carriages, silent, sad, moist-eyed; they looked at the tiled and the red tin roofs as they were left behind in the distance, vanishing into the valley whose forested slopes were clad in rust-red autumn leaves.

*La divisione Vesuvio* arrived at the Ukrainian front. And in the winter of 1942, at the Don-river Bend, the whole division was wiped out.

The army, it is true, was well equipped, with modern artillery, armoured cars, heavy shells and ammunition aplenty, but the Italian soldiers did not have the right clothes for the Ukrainian winter, and they froze to death where they stood. When the Vesuvio division reached the front line, the OKW, that is, the Oberkommando of the German Wehrmacht, generously handed over to the Italians a section of the frontline, where, within weeks, most of them had lost their lives. For days and nights on end, the calm waters of the Don carried downstream the livid, frozen, mutilated corpses of soldiers in ragged grey-green uniforms. And among the lifeless bodies and the ice floes, there floated guitars and mandolins with broken strings.

In the same region of the Don, a little farther to the north, near Ostrogozhsk, Marcu Marcovitch, nicknamed Dox, because he read every issue of *The Adventures of Submarine Dox* and *Adventures of the Dox Crew*, also perished, as did Ebi Friedberg, whose widowed mother had wanted him to take over the running of the flour mill at Pecica, which was managed by distant relatives. Together with them perished their schoolmate from the economics school, Sárai Tibor, son of journalist Sárai Attila, author of *Élet Máramazosban*, or *Life in Maramureș*, who was set on becoming a doctor.

Marcovitch-Dox and Ebi Friedberg had been conscripted into a labour detachment, in which they wore their civilian clothes with yellow bands on their left arms and a *honved* cap, but without a rosette, as Jews were unworthy to wear the uniform and glorious insignia of the Royal Hungarian Army. The labour wasn't hard, you didn't have to dig trenches or break rocks with a pickaxe, because in fact it was a demining unit. The young men of that detachment were lined up in a closely packed row and sent to stamp across the field in front of the regular army so that they would detonate any mines laid by the enemy. Corporal Sárai Tibor, who had a gold-ribbon baccalaureate diploma, was one of the regular soldiers in uniform who followed the demining row at a safe, regulation distance, guarding them from behind with loaded rifle.

But by a twist of fate, Ebi Friedberg and Marcu Marcovitch-Dox did not die from a mine exploding beneath them, but in the same instant as Sárai Tibi, their guard, in an ordinary bombardment. Their camp took a direct hit from a heavy artillery shell just three days after they arrived at the front.

As soon as the official notification arrived, informing him that his son had 'died a hero's death for the Homeland on the Eastern Front', old man Sárai Attila, Tibor's father, who was a widower and had lived alone with his son, sat down at the large table of the editorial office, which was heaped with newspapers, cheap writing paper, bottles of ink, and photographic clichés, slowly pulled black sleeves over the cuffs of his black, threadbare jacket, and wrote the funerary announcement: 'With deep grief we announce the heroic death for the Homeland of Corporal Sárai Tibor, along with thousands of young Hungarian men on the Eastern Front…'

And every week thereafter, in a right-hand corner of the front page of *Élet Máramorosban* there appeared the same announcement, revised, improved, updated: 'Sárai Tibor, along with tens of thousands of young Hungarian men,' within a black frame that grew thicker and thicker. 'Sárai Tibor, along with hundreds of thousands of young Hungarian men…'

'The old man has lost his mind,' said the officials at the town hall and the town's military command. And they ordered that the old man be committed to the Sighet mental hospital.


Mrs Serena Tatzenhaus had every reason to be disappointed. She increasingly realised that these Hungarians, who had taken over northern Transylvania and Maramureş, were not the same Hungarians as in the time of Ferencz-Jóska.

In April 1944, one after the other, within the space of just four weeks, laws began to be enforced that were carbon copies of the Nuremberg Laws, with small local adjustments.

The Jews were no longer allowed to work as state functionaries or in the mayor's offices of towns and villages.

Jewish professionals – physicians, lawyers, engineers, dentists, and so on – were no longer allowed to practise.

Jews were not allowed to have maids, servants or domestic staff who were of pure Aryan origin.

In order to solve the 'Jewish problem,' they were to wear a yellow star at least fifteen centimetres in diameter from point to point, sewn to their chests and their backs; the telephone cables to their houses were to be cut and their radios were to be confiscated.

A law eloquently titled 'Law to Circumscribe the Supply of Foodstuffs to the Jews' was published, lest the category of citizen in question dare to eat more than their fair share of the wholesome bread of the Royal Hungarian State.

The Jews were not allowed to keep shops, restaurants or hotels. And so, just when business was picking up, the turn came for Mrs Serena Tatzenhaus, an admirer of the Hungarians from the time of Ferencz-Jóska, to surrender the Zona Hotel and Restaurant, along with the cash drawer she had guarded without much success, to a good Aryan-Hungarian from the town of Kaposvár, that he might contribute to the Aryanisation of Sighet.

But Mr David Josifovitch found a different solution. He surrendered the Tulip Pharmacy to a certain 'Strohmann,' a straw man, a pure-blooded Hungarian and old neighbour, who would pass as the owner in the eyes of the authorities.

Many others did the same, in tacit complicity with such straw men. But such expedients proved to be of very short duration. For the Jews had to vacate their homes, leaving all their possessions behind, and move to the ghetto on Tanners Street and Pointsman Lane and Snakes Street, the latter thus named because it snaked among numerous side-alleys.

A few weeks later, they were taken from the cramped houses of the ghetto and taken to the Makhzikei Thora Synagogue, which is to say, the synagogue of the Keepers of the Teaching, where they were searched by gendarmes with cockerel feathers in their caps and Hungarian state functionaries, who were looking for money, gold and jewels.

At the breast of Lucia Anghel, the daughter of the soap and cheese manufacturer, they found a ring of platinum with a diamond. Or perhaps it wasn't real platinum and the diamond wasn't genuine?

After this, escorted by the Hungarian gendarmes with cockerel feathers in their caps and armed with machineguns and spare magazines, they were taken to the goods ramp of Sighet station, loaded into seventeen cattle trucks with planks and barbed wire nailed over the ventilation windows.

On 16 May 1944, the first train of cattle trucks, packed with people, left Sighet station. In one of the trucks sat huddled David

Josifovitch, with his goatee à la Luigi Pirandello, Roza Josifovitch, as silent and frightened as ever, and their two children, Arnold and Elisabeth. Next to them on the floor of the cattle truck sat Mrs Amalia Anghel, a plump, chestnut-haired woman, still in the bloom of youth, Mr Maurice Anghel, a tall, sturdy, energetic, handsome man with a lined face, and their only daughter, Lucia.

It so happened that Arnold was sitting on the floor right next to Lucia. She kept her thin lips tightly shut and in the semi-darkness Arnold regarded her delicate profile. She had a long, slender neck, black hair gathered in a voluminous bun, and white, translucent skin; a profile worthy of an ivory cameo.

For three days and nights they travelled, with the train stopping at stations but seldom, and only for a short space of time.

Nobody knew where they were being taken. Before they left, it was rumoured that they would be put to work on the farms of the Hortobágy plain, replacing the peasants who had been sent to the front.

On the afternoon of the third day, the train stopped. And there it remained for hours. In the crowded cattle trucks, the air had grown stale. And it was hot, unbearably hot. Somebody managed to clamber up to the ventilation window, and peeping between the planks and barbed wire nailed over the opening, he managed to glimpse the sign on the front of the station building, spelling it out letter by letter: 'A-u-sch-w-i-tz!'

Nobody in the cattle truck had heard of such a place.

The whole of that afternoon they sat in the closed trucks. In the next truck along, huddled in a corner, sat Mrs Serena Tatzenhaus, next to her husband Mekil, who liked to play cards and rush around looking for business opportunities, their twin daughters, with their red hair and freckled faces, and their son Simion, who had made room next to him for Mrs Lina Friedberg, the mother of Ebi, with whom he had been at school. The old woman was all on her own and very short-sighted, and she had lugged with her a suitcase containing clothes, a teapot, a bag of sugar cubes, and the eiderdown quilt without which she couldn't sleep.

The train waited and waited, and Mrs Serena had time to think about how badly she had been mistaken. Those Hungarians were not the same as the ones from the time of Franz-Josef. And how she had rejoiced when that admiral, who had once been the adjutant of the Emperor himself, had entered Baia Mare on a white horse. It was rather ridiculous, an admiral-horseman triumphantly entering a town conquered by negotiation and chancellery documents, but she had genuinely rejoiced. 'How the world changes and how much people can change in the space of just thirty years,' Mrs Serena said to herself bitterly.

That evening, they heard the locomotive whistle and the creaking of metal as the train moved forward a few hundred metres.

The cattle trucks were abruptly opened, amid a deafening din.

'Out! Out! Quick! Quick! Leave your luggage!'

The spotlights blinded their eyes.

'The women separately from the men!'

A truncheon pointed the direction: to the left … to the right …

# The Secret Mission

In the few days that had elapsed since the ghetto was set up in the little Carpathian town of Ostrov, the Jewish council, the so-called Judenrat, had succeeded in being neither good nor bad, but rather in being wholly naïve.

Appointed chairman of the council, Mr Faivel Fischknopf was an elderly Jew with a little pointed white beard. Just a few days previously, before being sent to the ghetto, he had been the owner of a haberdashery and dress shop, 'Glove & Cane', which had been taken over by a moustached man from across the Danube, after he had proven to the authorities, God alone knows how, that pure Aryan blood had flowed in his family's veins since the time of his great-great-grandfathers, since the days of Attila, Tass and Töhötöm.

The chairman of the Jewish Council was therefore Mr Faivel Fischknopf, but from the very start its driving force was Moti Orentlicher, nicknamed Motke, a short, swarthy little man, with beady, badger's eyes, a lively, enterprising travelling salesman, who had travelled all his life, selling all kinds of goods, so much so that you would have been hard put to list them all. In his time, he had sold every kind of paste, cream, powder: toothpaste, shoe polish, brass polish, washing powder. For a time, he sold various small textile products: handkerchiefs, shawls, washcloths, napkins, towels, head-scarves. Another time, he had travelled with samples of alcoholic beverages: wines, liqueurs, slivovitz, this being perhaps his merriest period, since on his return he had used to taste the little sample bottles that remained in his valise, after which he would loudly tell jokes in his third-class compartment, and laugh and sing, thereby enlivening the whole of the crowded train carriage.

Well, on finding himself shut up inside the walls of the ghetto, this Motke Orentlicher had to find some way or another of releasing his pent-up energy. And he did so by tirelessly running back and forth all over the ghetto, dispensing advice left and right on how to keep the streets clean, on how to dispose of the waste, and more particularly, he would visit the Jewish Council three times a day, each time bringing a new idea.

His ideas were very good, there was no denying it, they were acceptable and even accepted, on the one side. On the Jewish side. For example, one day Orentlicher came up with the idea of distributing a chocolate bar to each child in the ghetto every Friday. The idea was deemed excellent and unanimously accepted by all the councillors of the Judenrat. So the idea was passed, there were children aplenty, but where was the chocolate?

Another time, Orentlicher proposed that a corridor for the Jews be made, like the one in Danzig, which is to say, that two side streets be authorised to allow the Jews to circulate freely as far as the Mental Hospital, where seventy-five Jews were interned, so that they could take them Jewish food, cholent and kugel, at least on the Sabbath. The proposal was enthusiastically accepted by the Judenrat, Mr Faivel Fischknopf, the chairman, even praised Motke Orentlicher for it, smoothing his pointed little white beard in satisfaction, the motion was passed, there were patients aplenty, but there was nobody to listen to the proposal: the town hall and the local police, which guarded the ghetto, gave orders, but they didn't listen to even the most just and sensible Jewish proposals.

But you have to give Motke Orentlicher his due. Once, just once, one of his proposals was accepted, passed, and successfully put into everyday practice.

The ghetto's Jewish Council received from the town hall lists of the Jews that had to be put to work, along with where they had to work. The ghetto therefore sent one hundred and fifty men to the railway depot to load coal into the locomotives' tenders, three hundred and seventeen men were set to build dykes along the River Inar, two hundred and thirty-four men were sent to break rocks to build the highway north of Ostrov, and so on. The list also demanded that two Jews daily present themselves at the Villa Rosa on Linden Street, No. 14, where a number of SS soldiers from the SD, i.e. the Sicherheitsdienst, or Reich Security Service, were quartered. The two had to be there at seven on the dot every morning to pump water to the villa's kitchen and bath.

The Judenrat was about to send two stout fellows, butcher's apprentices, but Motke Orentlicher jumped up as if scalded and loudly cried, 'No! I object!' Then, in a low, almost conspiratorial voice, he went on: 'To do this job we need to send two intelligent men who speak fluent German. Understand? They need to have a fine nose… To sniff out what's what there… To eavesdrop, maybe we'll find out something in advance…'

And Motke meaningfully blinked his beady, badger's eyes.

The motion was passed and at the same meeting, the two 'pump men' for the Villa Rosa were decided upon: Mr Mark Holoker and Lucian Bercu, a student. The two were like Laurel and Hardy, and then some. Holoker was very short and stocky, almost completely round, with a round head framed by a round ginger beard and a hat with a brim stitched à la Eden: he was a trader in horses' oats, and had formerly done business in Germany. Bercu had blond hair, which he wore swept up, was as tall as a pike, and had a long throat, up and down which bobbed an Adam's apple like a ping-pong ball. Lucian had been studying chemistry at university when he was sent to the ghetto.

At seven in the morning, on the dot, the two arrived at the Villa Rose, Linden Street, No. 14. A nondescript, expressionless SS soldier let them in. But how were they to smell anything? How were they to eavesdrop? They didn't see a single SS man the whole day, let alone hear a single word of German. The pump was in the yard, a hand pump. The water was pumped up to a large cistern in the attic of the villa. When it was full, the water gushed down through a pipe under pressure.

The pumping, which the two took in turns, was by no means an easy task. The two sturdy butcher's apprentices would have been better suited. Mr Mark, with his à la Eden hat on his head and his patterned tie around his neck, sweated profusely and panted noisily, like a pair of bellows, and the young Lucian, thin and as long as a day of fasting, also breathed heavily. He had been twice given a postponement for national service due to anaemia and Basedow's disease, or 'incipient goitre', as his medical report put it.

When the two returned to the ghetto after their first day's work and told everybody that there was nothing to tell, that they had seen and heard nothing, the Council could not hide its disappointment and looked at Motke Orentlicher askance. But Motke was undeterred. 'It's only the beginning, let's have a little patience, gentlemen, we'll see later on,' he said, blinking his little badger's eyes meaningfully.

And he was right, that Motke. About two days later, as the two men were pumping and sweating away, an old soldier suddenly appeared from the kitchen, a one-eyed man with a bony face, who, without a word, gave each of them a very thin slice of bread and marmalade. Starvation had yet to strike the ghetto and when the two told of the slices of bread they had received, Orentlicher triumphally cried, 'I told you! It's a good sign. It means their intentions for us are not bad…'

And chairman Faivel Fischkopf smoothed his pointed little beard, and the other councils nodded their heads in satisfaction.

After another two days, they found out more. Leaving the gate of the villa, Lucian had almost collided chest to chest with a young

SS officer. For a few moments they stood face to face, both of them lanky, both blond, thin, but one in shabby civilian clothes, which hung loosely from his body, the other in a crisp, carefully brushed green uniform, with a diagonal chest strap and service revolver, with highly polished boots.

'*Was*?' exclaimed the officer with a frown, looking at Lucian's blond hair. 'What? Haven't they cut your hair? Hasn't the order reached the ghetto yet?'

And without waiting for a reply, he quickly went inside the villa.

The two hastened to take that snippet of information to the ghetto. And it was true, that very afternoon, two policemen on motorcycles brought the order. Every man, woman and child in the ghetto had to shave their heads.

Motke Orentlicher rubbed his hands in satisfaction: 'You see, we knew in advance…'

But half an hour later, the two policemen on motorcycles brought another order. Nobody in the ghetto was to be shorn.

Orentlicher was jubilant: 'Didn't I tell you? They don't have any bad intentions for us, after all…'

About a week later, the head of every man, woman and child was shaved at Auschwitz.

All the Jews from the ghetto of Ostrov, the town in the Carpathians, were taken away in four transports of three thousand each, seventy people to a cattle truck.

In the final transport, in the lead cattle truck, chairman Faivel Fischknopf, Motke Orentlicher and the other members of the Jewish Council, the so-called Judenrat, sat on the floor next to the pail of water and the toilet bucket. And transported in the rear cattle truck were the seventy-five patients from the mental hospital.

Three days later they arrived at Auschwitz.

None of them, neither the mental patients nor the mentally sound, not even Motke Orentlicher, had ever heard of Auschwitz before.

# The Rabbi's Beneficent Beard

It would seem that the good world is made up of two kinds of people: good Jews and good non-Jews. As for the bad ones, it's not worth talking about them.

Dr Emilian Dorna was without doubt a good non-Jew, or, as they say, a highly decent 'goy'. He was the son of a peasant ploughman from a village in the Maramureş Carpathians, as tall and as straight as a fir tree: his back was broad, the skin of his face was tanned, he was clean-shaven, his lips were fleshy, his nose robust, slightly pink, like a superior variety of red potato, his eyes dark, glinting beneath heavy eyelids. At the age of seventy, he still looked like a hale and hearty peasant, who did not seem all too comfortable in his elegant German suit. His curly hair, as stiff as wire, had lost its former blackness and was now as brilliantly white as the snow of the mountain peaks among which he had grown up.

Dr Dorna was, therefore, a decent 'goy'. It was even rumoured that during the war he kept perfectly healthy Jews in hospital, in the venereal and contagious skin diseases ward, of which he was in charge, thereby saving them from deportation to the concentration camps. He never talked about that. But once, bumping into him on the street and chatting to him about this and that, I alluded to his praiseworthy deed when the subject turned to those times. He gave a mysterious smile, grasped my arm, and said:

'Not so fast! Don't be hasty to pass judgement! Let me tell you the whole story from beginning to end, and then you'll see whether it was really my own merit… It all started with the rabbi's beard…'

My open-mouthed surprise must have been all too obvious, for Dr Emilian Dorna's dark eyes twinkled mischievously beneath their heavy lids, he took me by the arm and led me to the terrace of the Three Firs restaurant.

'A bottle of Cotnar!' he ordered curtly. The waiter quickly brought the tawny wine and two glasses.

The doctor drank from his glass thirstily and continued:

'Yes, yes! It all started with the rabbi's beard. You know, from my village, Poiana-Verde, I went to the capital to study to be a doctor… In my final year at medical school, one of my professors was Dr Coriolan Teutoniu, a specialist in venereal and skin diseases, an important man, a famous scientist… Back home, I left behind my father and elder brothers to plough the fields; I left behind my mother and sisters to tend the vegetable patch. For six years, I scraped by on meagre grants and giving private lessons; I lived on bread and onions, and from time to time a hot broth at the canteen, until finally I became a doctor. I settled here, in this little town of ours in the foothills of the mountains where my village lies… And before long, I married, started a family… By then I was a wealthy man…'

'And, of course, your lady wife contributed her dowry.' I ventured to remark.

'Not at all!' the doctor laughed cheerfully. 'She was the daughter of down-at-heel landowners from Moldavia. I met her when I was a student, in the capital. She was studying piano. But it was not at all hard for her to give it up for a peasant like myself… Not only was I a handsome, athletic young man, with a parchment diploma hanging on the wall, but after only a few years as a practising doctor,

I was famous, I was rich, I had my own house, with a six-cylinder chauffeur-driven Ford motorcar waiting outside…'

Dr Emilian Dorna smoothed his white hair, as stiff as wire, and went on:

'How did it all come about, you'll likely want to ask? After all, everybody knows how hard a young doctor has to work before he manages to build up a list of patients… Well, in my case, I think it was a kind of miracle…'

The doctor paused, smiling as if at the memory.

'A miracle?' I timidly asked.

'Yes, well, I can't think of a better word for it… It so happened that the chief rabbi of our little town, Moshe-Chaim Rottenburg of Ostrov, started to feel an itch on his chin: a skin infection underneath the handsome blond wavy beard that rippled down over his chest. It stung badly, the rabbi couldn't stand it any more, he constantly felt the need to scratch his beard, which was not only unpleasant, but also highly inappropriate for a man of his position… Well, what does a chief rabbi do when he has an itch? He goes to the doctor. But not just any provincial doctor. At the recommendation of his congregation, many of whom were wealthy, influential men, he went to see a famous doctor, a great specialist in skin diseases. And so it was that the great rabbi of Ostrov, accompanied by a *pamalie*, that is, a retinue of trustees, ushers, and other quite simply faithful parishioners, who followed in his footsteps everywhere he went, arrived in the capital to see the famous Professor Coriolan Teutoniu. Obviously, it wasn't hard for the professor to make a diagnosis: a common or garden fungus, a skin infection. To treat it locally, externally, the rabbi would have to shave off his beard…'

Dr Dorna paused, slowly sipped the glass of tawny wine in front of him. He then continued the story:

'You understand? The great rabbi Moshe-Chaim Rottenburg of Ostrov and its environs would have to cut off his beard. The golden-blond beard that rippled down over his chest… I should tell you from the very start, lest you labour under any suspicion, that Professor Coriolan Teutoniu – I was his student and I knew him well – was a cultivated, enlightened man, without prejudices, without superstitions, and he had nothing against rabbis, priests, preachers or other servants of the Lord Above, be they bearded or un-bearded… Perhaps, given he was a man with a sense of humour, he will not have been able to resist bragging in company, particularly in the company of beautiful women – Professor Teutoniu was a great womaniser – to the effect, 'Ladies, you are going to see something marvellous: I am to cut off the beard of the great rabbi of Ostrov.' A piquant situation, as you can imagine. Perhaps the professor even made a wager on it… Well, if he made a wager, know that he lost! As soon as he heard about cutting off his beard, the rabbi ordered his suitcases to be packed again and, with his entire retinue of trustees, ushers and the other quite simply faithful parishioners and followers in his footsteps, quickly returned home.'

Dr Dorna crossed his eyes slightly as he looked at the tawny liquid in his glass and smiled at the memory:

'It was a hot summer day. I was sitting in my surgery, in a house on the edge of town, where the rent was cheap – two rooms: a bedroom and a simulation of a surgery, with a small vestibule cum waiting room in front – I was sitting at my desk, watching the flies as they buzzed impertinently around my head, when all of a sudden, two respectable gentlemen came in, trustees of the Independent Orthodox Jewish Community, as they were called. I had been summoned by the rabbi of Ostrov. And so off I went. And I saw what was what. Unlike Professor Coriolan Teutoniu, I had time and patience aplenty. The patients weren't crowding my two-metre-square vestibule… and so I could localise the spots that were infected. Then, with a pair of tweezers, I carefully plucked strands of the beard from one small area of the infected skin. I plucked the hairs one by one, so that it wouldn't hurt very much, and applied an ointment. Then, a few days later, I plucked some more strands in a different spot and applied the ointment. I harried the infection like that until it began to retreat. The itching ceased. And after a few weeks, the skin was healed. Not a trace of the infection. And the blond beard of the rabbi, which cascaded so proudly over his chest, remained visibly intact…'

Dr Emilian Dorna blinked merrily.

'As you can imagine, from that day forth, the word began to spread. That I was a good doctor, skilled, conscientious, and so on and so forth… After a while, my fame became awkward, ridiculous even. Not without provincial pride, not without local patriotism, people boasted that 'our' Dr Emilian Dorna had succeeded where the great professor from the capital had failed… You understand? A veritable nightmare. And I couldn't shake off the rumour. No matter how hard I tried, no matter how much I denied it, no matter how much I implored: 'Good people! Gentlemen! It's absurd; it isn't true!' To no avail. It even had the opposite effect: 'How modest our doctor is,' they would say, now even more admiring. And they added my modesty to my merits… As you know, public opinion can raise you from nothing to as high as the seventh heaven, and it can also cast you down into the dust for no reason at all, it can trample you underfoot without mercy… And so, my fame spread, and patients came to me from all over town and the nearby villages, and even from other, nearby towns. My patients included the county prefect, the town mayor, the chief of police, the chairmen of benevolent societies, their families, the whole of the town's elite… Needless to say, I continued to be physician to the family of the Rabbi of Ostrov and his parishioners from the town and its environs. Patients even came to me from faraway lands, from over the ocean, since the rabbi had many followers around the world… That was how I became a famous doctor, with his own house and surgery, with all the latest instruments and equipment, both necessary and unnecessary, and with a chauffeur-driven six-cylinder Ford motorcar at my disposal. And I was able to afford the luxury of marrying the daughter of down-at-heel landowners, a piano teacher, whom I met as a student…'

The doctor smiled, sipped his glass of Cotnar wine. Then, a shadow passed over his tanned face:

'But the story of the rabbi's beard did not end there. For, you see, I was the one who saved his beard, but in the end, I was also the one who had to cut it off…'

Seeing the amazement, the consternation, on my face, Dr Dorna went on:

'Yes, yes! With my own hand, I cut off the stately, rippling, blond beard. And there was no infection; his skin was smooth, clean, healthy. But the world around us was infected. By hatred. An evil fungus, which had spread as far as our little town… I first cut off his beard with a pair of scissors, leaving the moustache, then I shaved him with a sharpened sliver of wood – it was forbidden for a razor to touch the beard… Neither of us spoke. I saw his eyes overflow with the tears he had been holding back; he saw the tears hanging as if frozen in my eyes… With his shaved chin and bushy, walrus moustache, he looked like a genuine 'goy', like a good Orthodox Christian… I obtained documents for him and filled out a medical record slip in the name of Pavel Stancu, a farmer from the village Poiana Verde, and I admitted him to the venereal and skin diseases section of the hospital, of which I was in charge. With him, I admitted another six members of his congregation, officially wanted as evil-doers, without their ever having done evil to anyone. I put them in isolation in a ward of the contagious diseases section, hanging a sign on the door: 'No entry! Highly contagious!' I don't need to tell you how terrified I was for them. And for myself equally so… A single denunciation, a single inspection, and it would have been over for them. And for myself… There even was an unannounced inspection. A commission headed by one of their superior officers, a doctor, whose rank was 'SS-Hauptsturmführer' My heart shrank to the size of a flea. The SS doctor was very *'höflich'* very polite; he addressed me as *'Kollege', 'Herr Kollege'* this, *'Herr Kollege'* that… Luckily, he couldn't be bothered to visit the 'highly contagious' ward, and contented himself with hearing my detailed account, peppered with scientific terms… Imagine if he had walked in on my 'Christians' wrapped in the tallit, in their prayer shawls, rocking back and forth as they murmured their morning prayer… I myself walked in on them like that countless times… I was lucky. Or maybe the Lord Above protected me for not having cut off the rabbi's beard. And for cutting it off… Who knows? The fact is that after the war, the beard grew back and Rabbi Moshe-Chaim Rottenburg of Ostrov went to the Holy Land, having gathered those of his parishioners who had survived the camps, and there he founded a large synagogue and schools for children, and schools for craftsmen, and benevolent societies. And he died a good death, if such a thing exists, at the age of ninety-three…'

Dr Emilian Dorna made a long pause. Then he concluded curtly:

'Well, that is the story of the rabbi's beard.'

And he drained the last drop of tawny wine from his glass.

# A Slice of Bread

Terrible cold, hunger. A persistent, nagging hunger. Like a relentless, evil spirit, which leaves you not a moment's peace. It prevents you from thinking about anything else. It doesn't prick you with a pin, it doesn't cut you with a knife, it doesn't hit you over the head. You're merely hungry. Hungry. Hungry.

In the round hut, with the tapering walls and roof, made of thick green-painted cardboard, in the labour camp on the Wolfsberg, which is to say, Wolf's Mountain. The camp is part of the Grossrosen cluster of concentration camps. The administration, the organisation, the execution of orders is flawless. Each inmate has received a striped uniform, like a pair of pyjamas made of stiff cloth, a cap made of the same material, grey with dark blue stripes, a tin plate and spoon, and a number. Which is to say, each has become a number.

And these numbers sleep in the round huts that form the perfect rows of the camp. Number 37013, curled up with the black blanket pulled over his head, cannot sleep. The hunger nags him. A dull, agonizing hunger. And in the straw at the head of his bed is a bread ration. A dense slice of soya bread. Every evening, after he comes back from his toil at the labour site where they are building a railway through the mountains, he receives a slice of soya bread and an extra, a cube of margarine substitute or marmalade. Every day, number 37013 eats all his bread and the *zulag*, the extra. And he sleeps like the dead. The next day, at the crack of dawn, when the prisoners receive their 'coffee' – water muddied with a kind of coffee substitute – he has not one crumb of bread left.

And so, he has made a firm decision. He will leave half his bread ration for the next day. And the slice of bread is beneath his head, in the straw, ten centimetres from his mouth. And the hunger torments him, nags him. He cannot fall asleep. Is it midnight? Maybe it is past midnight. An eternity. When will morning come? Not for an eternity will morning come… He stretches out his hand, rummages in the straw beneath his head. Yes, it's still there. He takes out the bread and begins to gnaw it. He eats it. All of it. To the last crumb. And he sleeps like a log.

A few days after that, at the labour site, he saw that one of the prisoners had a pencil. Good God! A pencil! Actually, it was the stump of a thick carpenter's pencil. But a pencil nonetheless, with which you could write. With which you could put down a thought on a piece of thick paper torn from the sacks of cement. The haggling began. A quarter of a bread ration for the pencil. The other number demanded the whole ration. Do you want to kill me? Should I go a day without bread? The other man agreed to receive payment in two instalments. No, half a ration, and that's final. More than that would be impossible! He bought the pencil and the very same day, during the brief meal break, after the thin gruel, he wrote on a piece of paper from the cement. What did he write? He doesn't even know any more. Something very important, obviously.

And that evening, after he received his bread ration, he carefully cut half a slice of bread and paid for the pencil. And the other half he ate straight away, along with the cube of margarine substitute. And the whole night he slept like a log.

Line up! March! They go down into the valley, to Wustegiersdorf, to the bath. A long barrack. At one end, they get undressed. Stark naked, living skeletons, they pass under the shower. They come out at the other end of the long barrack. Here, each receives another striped uniform, reeking of disinfectant. The old uniforms are left behind. Along with his pencil and the scraps of paper from the cement on which he has scribbled. What was written on them? Who knows? Very important things, obviously.

# The
# Old Paper
# Factory

They were sitting in a beer hall on thick benches, at a table of solid oak, stained and blackened by age. They were drinking from earthenware mugs and looking out of the wide window at the narrow, two- and three-storey houses on the other side of the street, which were pressed up against each other, each with its small square and rectangular windows, and a tall, tapering roof.

'This place seems terribly familiar!' said Rosa.

'Yes, it does,' agreed Clara, softly.

'It's only natural, given that just yesterday we passed through a number of little towns that looked more or less the same as this one,' observed Yoram Hartov, ironically. 'All these little German towns look as alike as two droplets of German lager beer!'

In all his half century of life, Yoram Hartov, born and bred in Rishon LeTsiyon, a farmer with vineyards at the edge of Rishon, had never left his native Israel till now. Only now, after seventeen years of marriage had his wife, Rosa, managed to persuade him to see a little of the world, in other words, to take a trip to Europe. With Clara, Rosa's childhood friend, and her husband, Arthur Willkind, a district magistrate in Tel Aviv, they had flown to Amsterdam, where they rented an Audi motorcar and set out across Germany, Switzerland and Austria.

'What's the name of this town?' asked Rosa.

'Let me take a look at the map,' said Arthur Willkind, who had taken on the role of guide, having travelled to Europe before, and quickly opened his leather map case, of which he was very proud. He had had it ever since he was an officer in the Jewish Brigade, when he fought in Italy.

Art traced their route with his finger over the map.

'We set out from Salzburg this morning, which is here, and headed toward Lake Attersee, and now we're in Len… Lentzing-an-der-Oberdonau.'

'What? Lentzing, you say?' stammered Clara, his wife. She turned pale and her green eyes suddenly blazed. She looked at her friend, wide-eyed, troubled. 'Lentzing… Did you hear that, Rosa? We're in Lentzing…'

'I heard.'

'The *alte Papierfabrik*!'

'I remember, Clara!'

'What does that mean?' asked Arthur.

'The old paper factory. We have to go there, Art!' said Clara imploringly.

'I wouldn't even think about it!' snapped Yoram Hartov. 'I have no interest whatsoever in ruined old paper factories. We've got enough ruins in Israel as it is… And besides, we have to arrive in Gemmunden before nightfall. We reserved rooms at the hotel there.'

'We have to go there, we have to go to the *alte Papierfabrik*… we have to… we can't not go…' murmured Clara, as if she hadn't heard what Yoram said.

'We were held prisoner there during the war,' Rosa tried to explain to her husband.

'So what? It was a long time ago! It's time that you forgot, don't come to me with those stories about…'

A sharp glance from Rosa cut off her husband Yoram's words. 'Then, let's go there,' said Art Willkind.

He folded up the map, closed his map case, and cried, *'Zahl!'*

He asked the waiter how to get to the old paper factory. The waiter, a tall, bony young man with a freckled face, paused to think: *'Meine Herren!* My grandfather once told me that there used to be a paper factory just outside the town, but I don't know where exactly… please forgive me.'

They went out into the street and climbed into their rented Audi. Soon they stopped to ask passers-by: 'Excuse me, which way to the *alte Papierfabrik*?'

A woman hurrying along with a carrier bag full of vegetables paused long enough to say, 'I don't know, I've never heard of it…'

A man in a black raincoat and black hat, with a black briefcase tucked under his arm, looking like an undertaker, courteously replied, 'Oh, I've heard of the factory, but to my deep regret, ladies and gentlemen, I don't know where it is…'

A grey-haired couple, both dressed the same, in suits of the same light grey material, smiled in embarrassment and answered in heavily English-accented German, 'Sorry! We're not from around here.'

An elderly man, short, fat, jovial, wearing a green Tyrolean hat, with a red moustache and Franz-Josef sideburns, exclaimed joyfully, as if hearing of an old acquaintance: *'Ja, ja, alte Papierfabrik…* Straight ahead till you reach Herder Strasse, then turn right, then left onto Engel Strasse, in fact no, first right, onto Heiligen Strasse, and the *alte Papierfabrik* is at the end.'

Art Willkind started the car. Yoram Hartov, in the passenger seat next to him, muttered something unintelligible from time to time. Sitting on the back seat next to Rosa, Clara gazed tensely out of the window without uttering a word.

Rosa could remain silent no longer: 'Every morning and evening we used to marched down the roads of this town, wearing grey prisoner's dresses sewn like sacks, our hair was cropped, as bristly as a hedgehog. And the girls from the town, nicely dressed, in clean clothes, with hats and shawls, with blond wavy hair falling to their shoulders, looked at us from the pavement, and we were ashamed. Why were we ashamed? I don't know…'

'Here's Herder Street,' said Art Willkind, peering at the sign on the corner. 'Now we turn right…'

'Then first on the right…' muttered Yoram Hartov, inwardly seething at this pointless detour.

'We marched in a column, in rows of five, a long column. Every morning we marched to the *Stollen*, the tunnels where we worked. They were digging tunnels into a hillside to shelter factories from the bombing. They laid dynamite, and then we removed the rubble from the tunnels, using *Lorre*, trolleys… Do you remember Herr Günther, Clara?'

Clara gave a vague smile, and Rosa continued.

'He was an elderly engineer, part of the Todd organisation, his name was Herr Günther, a mining engineer, and once he brought Clara a bar of chocolate. Do you remember, Clara? You gave me a piece.'

Clara nodded almost imperceptibly.

'One day, *Herr Ingenieur* Günther announced that we ought to receive milk! Every day. Because workers in the *Stollen*, underground, were entitled to receive milk by law. He even told the management, and after that I never saw him again… Nor did we see any milk… only that watery *Suppe*, a piece of soya bread, and the *Zulag*, a cube of marmalade, or margarine… Pfui, how hungry we still were, after we ate…'

There was silence inside the car. All that could be heard was the muffled drone of the engine.

'We're on Heiligen Strasse,' announced Art. 'Almost there!'

The houses grew fewer and fewer, smaller and smaller. They reached the end of the street. Willkind stopped the car. They all got out and looked around. An expanse of waste ground with sparse grass. The edge of town. No trace of a paper factory, or even the ruins of a factory.

'Maybe the factory was here and they demolished it?' asked Art Willkind.

'No, no, no!' murmured Clara in disappointment.

'There was never anything here,' said Yoram Hartov, and his red moustache quivered in annoyance.

'The factory wasn't here,' said Rosa. To one side of the old paper factory there was a hill with some young pine trees, and to the other side, there was a river… What was the river called, Clara, do you remember? It had a strange name: Taram… Taraum… no, it was Traun! Yes, Traun, that's what the river was called. And we called it the Traum, that is, the Dream… Because we dreamed of going to the river, of at least dipping our toes in the clear water. And we dreamed of climbing the hill, of sitting in the shade of the young pines. But we never did…'

'It's time to forget about dreams, Rosa, and to be on our way,' interjected Yoram, straight to the point. 'It will be dark soon and we have to check into our rooms at the hotel in Gemmunden.'

'I can't leave without seeing it… without having been there… I can't! I can't! I can't!' said Clara, overwrought, almost bursting into tears.

'Alright, alright,' said her husband reassuringly. Art Willkind looked like an English gentleman: tall, blond with greying temples, and he had an English air of calm; his having been a magistrate for the last thirty years helped him to be calm and patient.

Art questioned some more passers-by as to where they might find the *alte Papierfabrik*. Everybody had heard of it, but nobody knew where it was, or where it had used to be.

Finally, a man in blue overalls told them, 'I think the factory was demolished a long time ago. Anyway, it's not here, but on the other side of town, to the north. Take Grillparzer Strasse, then carry on down Apfel Strasse to the very end…'

They climbed back in the car.

'Clara was the youngest of us,' Rosa continued. 'She was fifteen. You should have seen her then, Art, with her pale, round face and burning green eyes, and her black hair bristling like a hedgehog… One night, I was asleep on the *kaya* – that's what we called the plank bunks – next to Clara, when I sensed her get out and slip outside. I paid no attention; I thought she must be going to the… to the toilet, which is what we called the latrine. Then, all of a sudden, shots rang out. We all leapt up from the bunks. A few minutes later, an *Aufseherin*, an SS woman supervisor, marched Clara back into the dormitory, holding her by the throat, she gave her such a loud slap across the face, it made her shake like a leaf in the wind, and then she sent her back to her place on the bunk… What had happened? In the middle of the night, Clara had set off up the hill to the young pines, the guard fired a few shots, an *Aufseherin* slapped her and brought her back. How lucky she was! Good God! They could have shot her… They could have hanged her for trying to escape… How lucky she was…'

At the end of Apfelbaum Strasse, there were vegetable gardens and farmyards as far as the eye could see, but no trace of a factory, of ruins, of a hill, of a river…'

'This is quite enough! Quite enough, I think!' said Yoram, and his thick red moustache quivered in annoyance. 'Let's be on our way and not look back!'

'I'm not going,' said Clara, her voice blank.

'Let's try again,' said Art Willkind, in a conciliatory voice. 'Don't you see, Yoram, that none of the locals claimed that there was never a paper factory here… Maybe we'll be able to find it… You know what, let's ask at the town hall!'

'The town hall, now, at half past five in the afternoon? Who in the world are you going to find at this hour?' asked Yoram, sarcastically.

'There must be somebody on duty!'

They went back into the town centre.

Clara was silent. Rosa, her childhood friend, couldn't stand the sullen silence inside the car any longer.

'We would march in a long column,' she continued, 'in our grey sack-like clothes, with our hair cropped, bristling like hedgehogs, we would pass through the town, and the young women on the way to their office jobs, the young women with the long, blond hair, would look at us from the pavement… Then we would leave the town and march down the road, crossing a railway line. We marched in a long column, five to a row. And one day, at dawn, it was misty, the air was opaque, milky, and a goods train appeared out of nowhere and mowed down one of the rows in the column, and we marched on… At first, nobody noticed that a row of five was missing. Only after the train screeched to a halt two hundred metres down the line, only then did they see the heap of limbs and skin and bristly heads that the locomotive had dragged down the tracks… They marshalled us into a column once more and we quickly marched away, in perfect formation, to our work in the *Stollen*, in the underground shafts…'

They arrived at the town hall: *Stadhaus – Lentzing an der Oberdonau,* said the Gothic letters of the sign above the door of the building with the tall clock tower, which showed that it was five to five precisely.

'*Keine Sprechstunden heute!* No more audiences today!' said the doorkeeper.

A woman was just coming out of the building. She was wearing a black widow's dress and a black hat with a wide brim, beneath which hung long wavy blond hair, falling to her shoulders. She was carrying a small briefcase. Presumably she worked there. She looked as if she might be the same age as Rosa: fifty-five. With her slender waist, blond hair, and winkles on her forehead and at the corners of her eyes, the woman even resembled Rosa.

On learning what the foreigners were looking for, she addressed the women in a sombre voice: 'The *alte Papierfabrik*? Then you were among the… oh, how sorry I used to be, when I saw them from the pavement, marching down the middle of the road, wearing those grey sacks, with their hair cropped, like hedgehogs… How sorry I used to be! But what could we do?' And then, addressing the men: 'Follow my car!'

They followed her black Opel. A few winding streets later, her car came to a stop, outside the town. She pointed to the spot and with a vague, embarrassed smile of farewell, the woman with the black hat and long blond hair went back to her car and drove away, in the direction of the town.

All four of them climbed out of the car.

Rosa and Clara looked around in silence. There was no paper factory or ruins, but only a stretch of uneven waste ground overrun with weeds. Perhaps the stones of the old factory lay beneath. On one side, there was a hill, but without any young pines. An asphalted road ran over the hill and it looked lower than it had then. And on the other side there was no river with swift, clear water, but a dry bed, with just a trickle of sluggish, dirty water, probably the run-off from some distant factory.

Rosa and Clara stood in bewildered silence.

Suddenly, Clara exclaimed, 'Do you hear it, Rosa?'

They both listened. From afar, from a house at the edge of town, could be heard the clanging of a piano. A child was playing *Für Elise*, slowly, awkwardly, just as someone had back then.

'It was here…' said Clara and set off to climb the hill, walking down the asphalted road. She stood at the top for a while, then turned around and softly said, 'We can leave now!'

She climbed into the back seat of the car without saying a word. Rosa sat down beside her.

Art Willkind started the car. Yoram breathed a sigh of relief: 'Finally!'

Clara fell asleep. The others could hear her breathing peacefully.

After a while, Yoram asked, 'Rosa, was that really the site of the factory?'

'No, no…' replied Rosa. 'That wasn't the river, nor was that the hill…'

They had left the town behind. The engine thrummed monotonously.

Clara slept. A sweet, peaceful sleep, like a child's sleep.

By the time they reached Gemmunden, night had fallen.

# The Coward

After he was born, finished his schooling, became a construction engineer, and, willingly and unwillingly, roamed foreign climes, Chaim-Hermann Hotiner finally returned to the land of his ancestors.

He arrived in Israel a few days before the New Year holidays, and on the evening of Rosh-Hashana he entered a synagogue. He had not set foot in a house of prayer for decades, and it all seemed alien and cold to him. The last time had been in the Etz HaChaim, that is, the Tree of Life house of prayer in the small town where he had grown up, he had listened to the Cohenites' prayer of blessing, hiding under his father's large *thalit*. It was warm and it was good beneath that prayer shawl with its four tasselled corners. The voices of the Cohenites had sounded familiar and yet mysterious in his ears, and he knew that they too were covered with the *thalit*, their hands raised to the heavens, their fingers spread in pairs, in a way that was mysterious, since you weren't allowed to look when the Cohenites blessed the people of Israel. And it was warm and it was good, and they all knew each other in that house of prayer, and they said to each other, '*A ghit yur!*' let it be a good year, with health, with joy, with *parnassa*, that is, with bread earned easily and honestly, and other such wishes.

But here, everything seemed alien and cold to him. That hexagonal synagogue, with its walls of concrete and glass that converged sharply to form a high ceiling, and a ceiling that seemed far too high and empty. The six walls of grey concrete, the white floor tiles, the people praying with elegant silk shawls casually draped over their shoulders, all of it seemed alien to him, and cold. But only for a few moments, for beside him he suddenly heard a voice: 'Would you like a *ma'hzor*?' And the man handed him a holiday prayer book.

Chaim-Hermann Hotiner gave a start. The voice sounded familiar to him, although he was sure he had never heard it before; that short Jewish man with the black-framed glasses and the short, neatly trimmed beard looked familiar to him, although he was sure he had never seen him before. Even the *ma'hzor*, the prayer book for Rosh-Hashana and Yom-Kippur, with its brown hardback covers, dog-eared in the corners, seemed familiar to him, although he was sure he had never held it in his hands. Nevertheless, that gesture, that moment, was one he had experienced somewhere before, in exactly the same way.

'Clean that window better!' said Dr Reichman, in a voice both imperious and imploring.

'But it's clean, doctor, can't you see? That's just frost-work. It's winter outside, doctor, can't you see? It's cold, doctor, can't you feel it?' And in his mind, Hotiner told Dr Reichman to go to hell.

Dr Moshe Reichman was a short man, with a black, neatly trimmed beard, and he wore thick, black-framed glasses. And he was a cowardly man, that Dr Reichman.

'Clean the damned window, clean it once again!' said the doctor, this time in a voice that was only imploring.

Hotiner gritted his teeth, with as much strength as remained to him … he tried to breathe warm air on the window and clean it. But it was hard for him to breathe any warm air. And Dr Reichman was a damned coward.

This was back in the winter of 1944, in the Zentral-Revier, the central infirmary of the Wüstegiersdorf concentration camp, in the middle of the snowy mountains, and the doctor was responsible for cleanliness and order in the infirmary. And it was well known that Cleanliness and Order there had to be! *Oberscharführer* Hopke, a commissioned officer in the SS, had made himself quite clear on that score. Only the other day, he had entered the sickroom and under the bed of one of the patients, a prisoner by the name of Mane Surkis, he had found two slivers of straw, presumably shed by his mattress. *Oberscharführer* Hopke had given the order that the offender's behind be given thirty strokes of the cane. The caned man had suffered a phlegmon, which is to say, the skin of his rump had remained intact, but pus had accumulated beneath; his buttocks had become two sacks of pus. The pus had then spread to the rest of his body. Dr Reichman and the infirmary's other medics had been able to do nothing except watch as the pus spread beneath the skin. Not that they would have had the wherewithal to do anything, or even to attempt anything. And a few weeks later, the man departed from among the living. It was in Poland, in the city of Lodz, where that very man had a textiles factory with five hundred workers, and his wife's parents had a textiles factory with two thousand workers, but all that was of no help to him.

'Please, Hotiner, clean the blasted window well! Please! Can't you understand I'm asking you nicely?'

A great coward, that Dr Reichman! Can't he see it's cold outside, and inside this crowded ward, the breath of sixty-six sick men means there's going to be frost-work on the window pane. It's not dirt, doctor, it's frost-work! You wipe it, you rub the pane with the cloth, and within five minutes, the frost-work appears in the corners again, starts spreading, nice and white. How are you supposed to heat this ward of sixty-six patients with just one bucket of briquettes a week? And the doctor doesn't even know that they burn planks from the beds in the stove, because it's so damned cold at night, here among these snowy mountains. And the planks holding up the mattresses have become perilously few, a lot of the prisoners sleep in precarious balance, on three planks, not daring to move in their sleep, lest they fall through the bed. It was damned cold and Hermann Hotiner was about to put another plank on the stove when somebody shouted, *'Achtung!'* in accordance with the procedure and they all froze in the positions they were in. *Oberscharführer* Hopke entered, tall, with a small head, his black hair glistening with cream, plastered across his brow, a carefully trimmed moustache above his thin upper lip, his black boots waxed to a sheen. He was followed by a short Jewish man with a carefully trimmed beard, with black-framed glasses: Dr Reichman, in charge of Order and Cleanliness. The *SS-Oberscharführer* made a slow circuit of the room and behind the stove he espied the bed board that had been about to be put in the stove. He erupted in fury.

*'Wie kommt das Brett hier?'* he yelled in a cracked voice, labouring each syllable. 'How did this board get here?'

Silence. They all froze, like statues in striped, prisoner's pyjamas. The officer opened the door of the stove. Then he made another circuit of the room, looking beneath the bunks. He now saw for himself what that wretched board was doing behind the stove.

*'Stubenälteste!'* yelled the SS officer. 'Who is the *Stubenälteste* around here?' Which is to say, the ward senior, a title that indicated not age, but responsibility.

'I am, *Herr Oberscharführer!'* answered Hermann Hotiner, pale, obedient, standing to attention, striking together the heels of his wooden clogs as hard as he could.

'Who did this?'

Frozen silence.

*'Stubenälteste!* I asked you a question! Who burned the boards in the stove?'

'I did, *Herr Oberscharführer!'* stammered Hotiner.

*'Dreissig auf den Arsch!'* shouted the officer. 'Thirty on the arse, with this board! Immediately!'

And the *SS-Oberscharführer* himself got ready to apply his sentence. Hotiner had to bend over his own bed and Dr Reichman had to count aloud the number of strokes the officer deftly delivered.

'One! Two! Three!' came the doctor's miserable voice.

But by a miracle, Hotiner barely felt any pain. First of all, the *Oberscharführer* struck not with the edge but with the flat of the board. Secondly, the blows were loud, but not very powerful. And after the fifth blow, the officer threw the board to the ground and went out.

'Don't burn any more boards! And don't leave any slivers of straw lying around! And clean the windows well!' pleaded Dr Reichman in a voice that was almost tearful, before quickly leaving the ward after the *Oberscharführer*.

A damned coward, that Jew, that Dr Reichman.

And on the night of Rosh-Hashana, the Jewish New Year, all the prisoners in the ward lay shivering in their beds, with their black blankets pulled over their heads. It was cold. Very, very cold. You had either to move or to sit still, with your knees to your mouth, covered in the blanket. But nobody had the strength to move.

Hotiner all of a sudden felt a hand gently touch him. He poked his nose from under the blanket. It was Dr Reichman.

'Would you like a *ma'hzor*?' the doctor asked him, as if it were the most natural thing in the world. And from beneath his striped coat he took a prayer book, with a brown hardback cover and dog-eared corners.

'What? A *ma'hzor*, here? Aren't you afraid, doctor? If they catch you, it's certain death...'

No, definitely not, Dr Moshe Reichman wasn't afraid. His eyes smiled at him calmly from behind the black-framed glasses.

Back at the synagogue, the short man with the untidily clipped beard, with the black-framed glasses, came to take back the *ma'hzor* after prayers. Later, Chaim Hotiner learned that his name was Hanoh Berkowitz, that he was a cobbler, and that on the Sabbath and high holidays, he was the verger of that hexagonal synagogue of concrete and glass.

# The Coffee Grinder

Liliana had everything she needed to be happy.

A home in a rectangular modern building situated at the angle where two streets intersected, a home consisting of two and a half rooms, plus bathroom, plus kitchen, plus larder, perfectly square, plus tiled toilet, square tiles in the kitchen, geometric parquet blocks in the other rooms; and modern, rectangular furniture throughout.

Within just a few years of marriage, the house was filled with more and more practical, highly useful things: a radio, a television, a stereo record player, a washing machine, a vacuum cleaner, a refrigerator, a kitchen appliance that blended, squeezed, mashed, sliced, diced, whipped, and performed all kinds of other actions. Everything worked soundlessly. There would be a slight buzzing, like a bee, nothing more. Her husband, who was an electrical engineer, highly capable and enterprising a young man, had seen to everything. They had married for love. They both earned good money, she had studied decorative art and worked as a designer for a fashion house, and was recognised as one of the best when it came to op-art patterns for dresses and objects. She was mad about geometry. Thanks to her husband, who saw to the maintenance of the domestic appliances, everything worked perfectly. He even set up a system of differently coloured wires, which fanned out through the house like nerves before bunching into a single braid, so that the radio, the record player and the television set could be operated by remote control, and could be turned on and off from anywhere in the house, from an armchair in the living room, from the bed in the bedroom, from the kitchen, from the toilet, merely by pressing a button on a portable panel the size of a handbag.

Liliana therefore had everything to be happy and nobody knew the cause of her quiet irritation, the symptoms of a strange illness that no doctor could begin to understand.

Maybe the coffee grinder was the final straw. Her husband had brought it for her when he came back from a trip abroad. It is possible, however, that anything else at all might have had the same effect on her. Liliana liked to drink coffee, and perhaps more than drinking coffee, she like to prepare it in her own special way. And her husband, wishing to make her happy, brought her a coffee grinder that ground the beans in precisely ten seconds, and if you let it grind the beans for fifteen seconds, it produced a powder so fine that it clogged up the orifices of the coffee maker. Actually, that ingenious coffee grinder didn't even grind the beans, but rather it spun them in a centrifuge with such force and speed that they were pulverised, they were smashed into tinier and tinier pieces. A faint hum, and the coffee was ready to brew.

That day, Liliana began to correct her husband's speech.

'Why do you say, "Make me a coffee, please, darling"?'

'Then how should I ask you?'

'Don't you see that "make me a coffee, please" is something sharp, with ten-degree angles, and "darling" is something round?'

'Are you serious, darling?'

'The circle again … Don't you see, Al, that we can't talk like that anymore? "I love you"… "I love you" is a triangle. Interesting! In the beginning, I'd thought it something round, round and colourful, like a child's ball. But no, now I realise it's a triangle … Every side is perfectly equal. Like this!'

And with her forefinger, she traced the lines in the air:

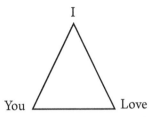

'Is that so? I'd never thought of it like that before …'

'And "I don't love you" is a square … Don't you feel it? A perfect square, like this:'

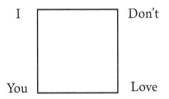

Her husband gave her a strange look. Then, with a laugh, he said, 'You're tired, Lili, let's go to bed!'

'All right, but on one condition, without the remote control. Let me get out of bed to turn off the television.'

She was quiet, but everything irritated her. An irritation that made her talk exaltedly, or to remain completely silent. But what irritated her more than anything else was that coffee grinder, perhaps without her realising it, but she didn't stop using it because she liked drinking coffee and the grinder was excellent. A ten-second hum and the beans were ground and ready for brewing.

In the meantime, her husband had started bringing a doctor to the house without her knowing it, he was a friend of his, in fact – they had been in the same year at university – a young specialist in internal diseases, who was now studying to specialise in psychology and psychopathology. He would come in the evening and as they talked he would sometimes ask the young woman a question, to which she would answer with a laugh, saying that she was perfectly fine, that sometimes she got headaches, above her eyes, that sometimes her vision clouded, probably because she was tired, but that she didn't need eyeglasses. The doctor prescribed her some painkillers, which she didn't take.

One evening, all three were drinking coffee and she was talking and laughing in a state of nervous irritation, when the young doctor, thinking to establish a patient history, brought up the subject of her parents. Liliana abruptly stopped laughing. She turned pale.

'What's wrong, darling?' asked her husband.

'It's nothing. It's been so long since I thought of them…' And after a long, oppressive silence: 'Forgive me. I'm tired. I want to go to bed.'

The doctor took his leave.

The couple went to bed, without turning on the television, without playing a record, without listening to the radio. For a few hours, she tossed and turned in bed, then fell asleep, exhausted. In the morning, she told her husband that she had to go to the little town where she had been born and grew up. She no longer knew anybody there, but she felt the need to see that little town once more, the streets, the house where she once lived.

'Shall I come with you?'

'No, no! Go to the factory and arrange for me to have two or three days off.'

She put a few things in a valise and left.

From the window of the train carriage she saw the town in the distance. The three spires of the church. The tiled and the tin roofs. And at the edge of town, smoking factory chimneys and a row of tower blocks as if transplanted there from another town. The train came to a stop. The station had remained the same, but was now bustling with strangers. In her town, not one familiar face was waiting for her. Outside the station were three new taxis and two old horse-drawn cabs, with two old cabmen seated on the boxes. The so familiar streets! Look, there was their street. As a child it had seemed those places, the whole world was hers. After that, there was only the town, for war had come and you couldn't go anywhere else. Then that street of theirs had been blocked off, making it impossible to leave. At one end was a barbed wire fence and on the other side of it bayonets pointing at you. After that, only the street was hers and the sky above it. And the house, with all its nooks, with its dark cellar and its attic, with its mysterious lamps.

In their house a seamstress and her family now lived. What a coincidence! Her mother had been a seamstress too. But now the sewing machine wasn't so old. And the seamstress didn't sit in the same corner. It was an electric sewing machine, with modern, aerodynamic lines. Liliana looked at the seamstress, a fat, jovial woman, all smiles, and she apologised for bothering her and said in embarrassment that she had lived in that house once, long ago. The woman invited her inside, told her to take a seat, but Liliana remained standing. The woman told her she had been a seamstress, but she had three daughters and now she sewed only for the family. 'I have to sew for three girls, dresses and underlinen and everything, and then there are the household chores…' Her husband was a bricklayer and as it was summer, he came home late. She introduced Liliana to her daughters, the middle daughter was about the same age as she had been back then and it seemed to her that she resembled the girl she once was: eyes just as dark and her hair in pigtails. She wanted to see the kitchen and there, suddenly overcome by a strange faintness, she sat down on a stool without being invited, and she listened to the good woman's chatter, without understanding any of it. It was there that she had spent a part of her life, next to that slender woman in the cheap dress, rich only in the pleats in which it was so nice to bury your face. Her mother, who divided her life between the old, nimble Singer sewing machine and the clean, white kitchen, raising her little girl single-handedly after she lost her husband in an accident at the timber factory. Liliana remembered her father only very vaguely: just the outline of a broad-backed, taciturn man, who used to leave every morning. That was all. It was as if she always used to see only his back, as he left. But as for her mother, her mother was completely different. She was the hot milky coffee in the morning and the fresh buttered rolls and the warm hand that led her to school on her first day, leaving her at the gate, frightened, and waiting by the fence, with moist eyes, until, with the other strange and frightened girls, she went inside the tall grey building that inspired so much fear and respect. She would sit there, in the kitchen, on a stool, and look at her mother, as she went back and forth, busying herself in the other room, which was both a sitting room and a bedroom and a workshop. She would look at her mother's slender white hands as they softly pushed the cloth under the lively needle of the sewing machine. It was from her that she learned how to sew and make dresses, to create wonderful little dresses for her rag doll using coloured scraps. And when the street was blocked off and only the sky remained above them, a large family came to live in their house. There wasn't much room in their small house and that was why she and the blond little girl, who arrived with a swarm of little brothers and sisters, that was why she and her little blond friend, who was the same age as she, used to go up into the attic and stay there for hours at a time, sitting on a beam and talking and playing with the rag doll, putting it to bed, dressing it.

'I'd like to see the attic,' Liliana suddenly interrupted the spirited chatter of the fat, jovial woman, without realising what she was doing.

The woman looked at her in surprise, but without annoyance: 'Be my guest!' and wanted to accompany her.

'Please, don't trouble yourself!'

She went up on her own. The worn wooden steps groaned the same as they used to do, and the attic was the same. She sat down on a beam, on the same beam where she had used to sit with the little blond girl, when they played mother and aunt with the rag doll. They had dressed it, sent it to school, undressed it. They had told it to be good, they had put it to bed, told it, 'Good night, sleep tight'. Then they had used to climb up the beams and look out through the narrow little window in the red tile roof at the white and grey clouds that danced across the boundless blue sky. They would watch in wonder as the stars came out one by one. 'Look at the stars!' And above their heads there would shine a brilliant star, and the whole sky would be filled with stars and silence. All of a sudden, her mother's voice rang in her ears, calling her to come down, telling her they had to pack, they had to pack as much as they could carry. Her mother made her a nice bundle of blouses, dresses, her best shoes, all wrapped up in a tablecloth, and in her other hand she placed a basket of bread, cheese, and walnuts. In one hand, her mother held an old cardboard suitcase with worn corners, and in the other, a sack of pots and pans, which clanged every step of the way. Over her shoulders she carried a large bundle of clean sheets, two pillows, and a blanket, wrapped in another black blanket. They walked in silence, in a long line of sad, frightened people, old folk, women and children. They walked down empty streets to the station where the goods trucks were waiting, with planks and barbed wire nailed over their ventilation windows. She never knew how many days and nights they travelled in that crowded goods car. They finally disembarked without their luggage. 'Leave your luggage, you'll each get it back tomorrow morning!' somebody yelled as soon as the door of the car was slid open, its metal grating. They disembarked into the glare of a searchlight, her mother tightly clasping her by the hand, lest she lose her in that stream of people. The searchlights blinded them and they could barely see anything around them, they heard only the murmur of people and above the murmur the strident shouts, until a black truncheon divided her from her mother and pushed her to the right, and when her mother refused to let go of her hand, the man with the truncheon yelled, 'Tomorrow, you'll see her tomorrow morning!' and her mother went to the left, looking over her shoulder, and she watched until she lost sight of her mother in the crowd over which poured the silver-white blaze of the searchlights. The blinding light made her close her eyes. She opened them and looked around her…

The attic had remained the same. Yes, it was the same. The same cracked, time-blackened beams, above them the same rusted tin roof, the same old tins and boxes and bottles heaped in the corners. Maybe they were not the same ones, but they looked the same under their thick layer of dust. All of a sudden, her gaze fell on an object in one corner. Among the bottles and tin cans, she saw a coffee grinder. An old wooden coffee grinder. It was square, like a child's drawing of a house, with a drawer at the bottom and a dome at the top, from which protruded an S-shaped crank capped with a china knob. She rushed to pick it up, and blew the dust off it. She turned the crank, the grinder made a hoarse groan, then seized up. She turned the crank in the opposite direction and the box replied with a scraping, buzzing noise. It was a warm reply, which came from far away, from very far away. Liliana burst into tears. She wept, shaking.

When she finally came down from the attic holding the coffee grinder and asked the nice fat woman to let her keep it, the woman looked at her in amazement, looked at her reddened eyes, uncomprehending, but gave her wholehearted permission.


Liliana would sometimes forget and walk from the kitchen into the living room, milling coffee beans in the old grinder.

'How many times have I told you, Lili, that mill drives me out of my mind with its dreadful scraping noise,' said her husband, fleeing to another room.

But the dreadful scraping noise soothed her, in her ears it sounded like solemn music coming from somewhere far away.

Otherwise, it was the only bone of contention between husband and wife.

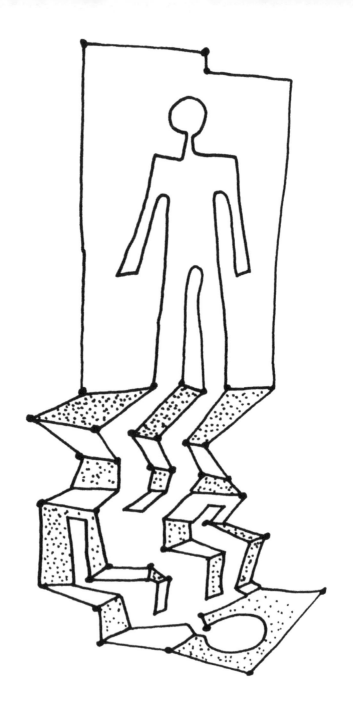

# The Death, Life and Birth of Dr Letoni

On Thursday morning, I get a telephone call from a friend: Dr Letoni is dead.

Unbelievable! I feel like somebody has hit me over the head.

Everybody used to talk about him and revile him and abuse him and curse him. They demanded a reckoning. Unanimously. And this is how he responds. Succinctly: he dies. Suddenly. Of a heart attack.

Nobody had been expecting such a response. He'd never been ill. And he'd seemed impervious.

There were a lot of people at the funeral. More than usual for so simple a ceremony. The people were pale-faced, astonished, as if they'd been hit over the head. Each felt something wasn't quite right, that things weren't the way they thought. That everything needed to be reconsidered.

At the burial, in front of the open grave, Dr Letoni, sleeping his eternal sleep, is witness to a final scene. His ex-wife and their two children are standing in tears when suddenly they notice the other wife, the doctor's present and legal wife, who, dressed in high mourning, has slipped her way through the throng, next to the deceased.

'Get out of here!' whispers the ex-wife, clenching her teeth.

'Why? He's my husband!' she growls back.

'Really? Then lie down next to him!' shouts the ex-wife. 'Go on, lie down next to him!'

Everybody turns pale, murmurs. The current wife quickly leaves, amid the murmurs.

By the graveside, his fellow physicians are giving orations. In each oration the same leitmotiv reoccurs, an idea about which nobody has thought lately, something completely forgotten: Dr Letoni was a good, an honest physician. Yes, caught up in their own private lives, people forgot that his whole life, this was an honest man, plain and simple. His modest, nondescript face, his watery, slightly bulging eyes, his rather tongue-tied way of speaking, none of this made you think of paying an honorarium or giving him something extra. After he examined you and then made his recommendations in a monotone, it was almost as if you didn't feel like putting your hand in your pocket. What is more, his modest face, his dull eyes, and his embarrassed smile, which accompanied you to the door, all seemed to be apologising for the fact that the patient had taken the trouble to come; they seemed to be thanking the patients for having given Dr Letoni the opportunity to examine them.

Yes, I forgot that detail. We all forgot it. As if we'd been ordered to do so. When he came to see me (actually, Dr Letoni only came to see me once, but how many times was I the one who went to see him?) on a certain matter, I gave him a cold but polite welcome. He came not for himself, but for his ex-wife, with whom he had had two children. It was a thorny problem: after he moved out of the building where, with his ex-wife and children, he had been a tenant ('After you left her and the children, the way you left her…' I said to myself, correcting him in my mind), she had had problems, somebody had bought the building, and now the new owner had found some clause or other in the contract, he was hell bent on evicting her and the children. 'That's because you left her defenceless, all by herself with the two children…' I added in my own mind. And now he had come to me, knowing that I was somebody important at the town hall, that I had a word to say when it came to the allocation of living space; he had come to me to ask me to help get her another flat, where she could have peace and quiet and the children would be able to do their schoolwork. Probably noticing my rather stony face, he raised his voice a little, only a very little, but even that was unusual for him; he said that I was obligated, that all of us in charge of the town's affairs were obligated to help a single mother of two children. The nerve of him! The blood rushed to my head and I yelled, 'You've no right to speak to me like that! You're the one who left her and the children…'

He was thunderstruck for a few moments and then, even more tongue-tied than usual because of his indignation, he said, 'What… what… what do you know? When you came to me with an ache or pain, I didn't speak to you like that… Never… never… never have I spoken to you like that…' And he left, with his head bowed, he left the way he had come, just as he usually walked, without his indignation causing him to lift his head in feigned pride.

Only now do I realise how right he was. What did we know about what had really happened? Everybody was talking about him, reviling him, abusing him, but as for knowing what really happened… Not so much. They knew only that he'd left his wife, not for the first time, abandoned her with two children, a boy of eight and a little girl of seven, and gone off with one of those women… Not to mention he was old… Almost sixty, or in his seventies, according to some… It was too much… But what did we know?

Again, it's true that when I came to him with my aches and pains, he didn't speak to me like that. He would listen carefully to my heartbeat, my lungs, he would take my pulse. He would give advice in his gentle, soothing voice; he would carefully write out the prescription in a neat, calligraphic hand, lest the pharmacist make a mistake. He had been an assistant bookkeeper before he packed that shabby cardboard suitcase he borrowed from his brother and went off to study medicine, and his professor at university, half joking, half serious, once told him that such legible handwriting was an affront to the medical profession Later, the apothecaries, probably annoyed at not having anything to decipher, made fun of him, saying that even a child at primary school would be able to read his prescriptions.

It was true, he never spoke like that when you went to his surgery, and after he gave you his prescription, you didn't feel like putting your hand in your pocket. It was as if his inscrutable, nondescript face rejected the gesture even before you made it. You didn't even feel like discreetly putting a little something on his desk or slipping a folded-up banknote in the baggy pocket of his white coat, either. Actually, I don't remember that clean, but rather rumpled, white coat even having pockets.

But now that he has departed so suddenly, I'm able to think clearly and I realise now how nicely he used to speak. What did I know? What did the others know? Or indeed, what did the whole town know, which gossiped about him, abused him, cursed him. Each of us knew a little something, but did we ever attempt, even if only in our minds, to put together what we did know about him… and only then to judge him? And then that tall, chestnut-haired girl arrived, the girl with the small round face, not very pretty, but young, very young; she arrived at the seventh precinct, looking for him. Her name was Olga, nobody knew her surname, but people didn't even call her that, they didn't call her Olga, but 'that girl'. And they used to say, 'so young but already a fallen woman.' But maybe they were exaggerating on that score too. But why did he have to marry her, hold a fancy wedding, as if she were an honest woman? People wondered, they were amazed, and they were angry, and they reviled him. And before his sudden death, it never crossed anybody's mind that maybe, just maybe, he did it because he was honest. Even if a strange honour, to leave a woman with two children for one of those women.

And what kind of life did they lead together, those two creatures not just from different worlds but different planets?

After he married her, he left that nice flat with its walnut furniture, its radio and television sets to his ex-wife and children, and he moved in with her, his new wife, in a small rented house at the edge of town, with one little room and a kitchen, with small, perfectly square windows and a ceiling with smoked beams showing. He was out all day, visiting his patients around the precinct. She spent very little time in the kitchen, she roamed around the town, doing the shopping, meeting all kinds of people in bars. The truth is, she wasn't much interested in men. She knew them all too well. To her, they were all the same, the differences between them were all too small. She wasn't interested in men, but when it came to drink, that was a different matter. People even used to say she drank like a man. And when she came home drunk, she would beat him. She would call him a ridiculous old man, an old crock. She would come home, singing snatches of old ballads: 'life is hell without you and moonlit nights', and when she saw him, she would yell at him, hit him, throw him out of the house in the middle of the night. His own house, since he was the one who paid the rent and the electricity and the heating and the broken windows, he paid for everything, everything… And when she fell asleep on the bed, passing out before she could get undressed or take her shoes off, he would softly, cautiously creep back inside, undress her, cover her up, lie down next to her. He liked that warm, supple body, its muscles now un-tensed, the sharp smell of strong perfume mingled with rum, muted by the smell of sweat. His sweat and hers. Lately, he had been running around and sweating a lot too.

How the hell had two people so different got together? That's what folk asked each other, without finding any answer. They knew only the facts, the petty facts, which came together in their minds only to unravel once more. Once, in the beginning, she came nicely dressed, as befitting a visit to the doctor, she came to the district seven dispensary with a cold or a stomach ache and she bared her breasts and he listened to her heartbeat, her lungs, he palpated her abdomen, on one side, above her hip, to see whether she had appendicitis. She came once, twice, three times. She was young, very young, tall, with a round face; he was a doctor, at the age 'just before the doors close,' as they say. And on top of everything else, he didn't get on with his wife, he sometimes quarrelled with her. Mara was blonde, blue-eyed, far prettier than that young woman, she was ambitious, and she had borne him two beautiful children, a little boy and girl. She was an ambitious woman, she was proud of being a doctor's wife, she always wanted something and once she got it, she wanted something else, and so she was never satisfied. She wanted to leave, to leave, to leave this place, this small provincial town, to live in a big city with wide streets and big, brightly lit shop windows. It was the shop windows that attracted her in particular. Not because she liked to buy things, she wasn't a spendthrift, but because she liked to look. She took great pleasure in looking at the lovely things displayed in the shop windows: dresses, handbags, umbrellas, shoes, especially the shoes. Whereas he, Dr Letoni, had been a physician his whole life, a modest, district physician. Even after he had his own surgery, with an X-ray machine and diathermy apparatus, he still had the soul of a district physician. But that's just a manner of speaking, because he never really had a surgery of his own, and the greater part of his life, he had been a district doctor, here in his home town, and also far away, in a mining town, which also had a carbon black factory, where in the morning you put on a white shirt and by evening it was black, where the dogs were black, the cows black, the hens black, where even the eggs turned black if you didn't eat them fast enough. And before that he had been a district doctor in a fishing village, where he visited his patients by rowing boat, after which, for who knows how many years, he returned to this small town in the mountains, where 'he first saw the light of day', and where he liked to live, not even he knew why, since he didn't find much joy here, unless it was simply because the air was clean and the water pure.

Mara, that blonde woman with serene blue eyes, that beautiful, ambitious woman, had had a single, stubborn, burning ambition from before she got married: to be a doctor's wife. Nothing except being a doctor's wife would do! And without hesitation, she took Dr Letoni from another woman, Serena, his previous wife, a doctor's widow, who, having lost her husband in the war, lived all alone in a big house with solid-wood furniture and its own surgery, with an X-ray machine and diathermy apparatus, the whole works. It was after the war. He returned home, single, without a surgery; she was single, without a husband, and had a surgery full of complicated equipment that was of no use to her. They married and lived in peace and harmony – although you can never know for sure what goes on within a marriage – until the blue-eyed blonde arrived. Probably with a cold or a stomach ache. He listened to her heartbeat, her lungs, took her pulse… He palpated her abdomen on one side, pressing lightly to see whether she had appendicitis… The girl came once, twice, three times, who knows how many times…

When somebody reproached the blue-eyed blonde, who had fulfilled her ambition of becoming a doctor's wife, for having taken him from another woman, leaving that woman all alone again with her surgery, X-ray machine and diathermy apparatus, she replied with the utmost sincerity: 'Is it my fault that I'm beautiful and she's not? That I'm young and she's not?'

It was true: Serena, the doctor's widow, whom Dr Letoni married after the war, was neither beautiful nor young. Some even said she was ugly, she had a coarse-skinned face and deep wrinkles under her eyes, her brown hair was wiry, frizzy, discoloured in places because of the curling tongs, which she used rather too often. On the other hand, Serena was an intelligent, well-read woman, who, once a week, on Saturday evening, received guests at her house for a game of rummy. Doctors, her husband's old friends, lawyers, school teachers, all of them serious men, accompanied by their well-built wives, used to come to play cards, drink tea, eat biscuits, and discuss the week's events. That was how Dr Letoni arrived at her house, at the invitation of a fellow doctor from the hospital, himself a habitué of Madam Serena's soirées. He came once, twice, three times, countless times, until he remained there permanently, in that house with its own surgery equipped with every instrument imaginable, including an X-ray machine and a diathermy apparatus. And they got on well, but after a time, her intelligence became rather tiring, and her increasingly frequent – they sometimes struck him as pointed – references to her first husband were downright irritating. Probably he cared about her greatly. More than he could show, but what was he to do? He had met her first husband before the war, he had met him during the war. A fleeting encounter, but in such particular circumstances.

He remembered that winter, when he had trudged those endless plains, swept by the icy north wind and deep in snow, wearing old boots wrapped in rags tied with wire. In the beginning, he had worked in the forced-labour brigade like all the others, breaking the frozen earth for artillery emplacements, chopping wood, laying railway ties and sleepers. Later, when the typhus epidemic had broken out, he had been taken to the dispensary to tend the sick, although there was not much he could do for them without medicines, without food, without the means to ensure basic hygiene. Lice swarmed everywhere, not even sparing the physicians. He had done what he could, until that cursed order for all the sick, as well as all those who were so much as suspected of typhus, to be transported to a central hospital specially fitted out for them. At first, they all rejoiced, physicians and patients alike: a hospital meant hygiene, medical treatment. It meant wards with whitewashed walls, beds with white sheets, nurses in white uniforms. But when he accompanied the first transport of twenty-nine patients with a high fever, riding with them on a truck covered with tarpaulin, there was no rejoicing when they arrived. Neither Dr Letoni nor the twenty-nine patients rejoiced when they saw that the 'hospital' was a long barracks, or rather a huge, rickety wooden shed, with a sagging roof of black shingle, which housed three-deep bunks made of dirty, un-planed planks, in which the sick were crammed like sardines, hundreds and thousands of them. A terrible murmur rippled from one end of the shed to the other, a mixture of groans, implorations and prayers, whose words were impossible to make out. But what troubled Dr Letoni even more were the SS officers who patrolled the environs, keeping a considerable distance between themselves and the shed lest they be contaminated. What kind of care would the sick receive there? Even the camp of the forced-labour brigade was a hundred times better. He would have liked to take his twenty-nine patients back in the truck, but it was too late. Harsh orders were rapped out, the sick men were unloaded from the truck and allotted bunks in the shed, amid the protests of those already there, who now had to cram together even more closely to make room for the newcomers. It was there that he met Dr Gottlieb, Madam Serena's husband, and they briefly exchanged a few words. How were they to treat the sick? With what? He didn't know either, for there were very few doctors… Dr Gottlieb's formerly rosy, round, jovial face was now covered with the stubble of a three-day beard; the skin of his face was dark and wrinkled like a dried prune. In any event, he said in a faint voice, they would do everything possible; they would attempt the impossible. Above all else, they would demand medicines. For the time being, there was nothing to be had there. Who knows what the gentlemen in charge could be thinking… He would demand suitable conditions… Dr Letoni then went to the commandant of the barracks – grandiloquently named the 'Central Hospital' – to inquire about how all those patients brought there from so many labour camps were to be treated and whether other physicians would be arriving. He volunteered to remain there himself in order to assist his colleagues, who wouldn't be able to cope with so many patients. The commandant, who received him on the steps of his office, some three hundred metres from the contagious wooden shed, looked at him for a few moments, smiling as if at a naïve child, or at least so it seemed to Dr Letoni, and then told him in a harsh, official-sounding voice that there would be sufficient physicians, that in any case it was none of his business, that his job was to bring the sick there, to make a head count, to countersign the delivery receipt, and that was all! Now that delivery had been made, he should make an about-turn and get the hell out of there! Understood? At which he marched back inside his office. The commandant's tone had struck Dr Letoni as strange at the time; it was as if he were hiding something behind that crassness, that harshness. Dr Letoni realised what it was only a few hours later, when returning along the deserted white road in the dark, the truck broke down and the driver cursed and swore because he couldn't manage to repair it. All of a sudden, they saw flames rise from the site of that huge hut. In the distance, they heard muffled cries and gunshots. The sky was red. The tinder-dry hut, lit from every side, was burning with all the patients and doctors inside. The gunshots were obviously intended for those who tried to escape through the smoke and flames. That was the point of the cordon of SS men. That was their way of eliminating the typhus epidemic. That night, Dr Letoni did not feel the cold, and by the time the driver repaired the engine, his toes were frostbitten.

He neither saw nor heard of Dr Gottlieb after that. He didn't tell Madam Serena anything. What would have been the point of aggravating open wounds? Or might he have mentioned something about it, long ago, during one of those soirées with tea and biscuits, between two games of rummy? What does it matter? And when Mara appeared in his life, that beautiful, blue-eyed, ambitious blonde, he left Madam Serena's house, he left the surgery, taking nothing, not so much as a pair of tweezers. They parted as friends.

And Dr Letoni went back to the seventh district, on the edge of town. His entire life, he had nothing, neither a house, nor a table, nor a surgery, nothing except his small surgical kit. He was nothing but a district doctor, but he was a doctor in the fullest sense, by vocation, body and soul. Before the war, he had been the local doctor in a fishing village, he had visited his patients by rowing boat, and his clothes had always smelled of fish and mud. The fishermen were good-hearted folk, patient and kind; they only ever fought on Sundays, when they drank. They were poor folk, they could give the doctor only what they had: their respect and a choice fish. But how many fish can a man eat?

After a few years, Dr Letoni was transferred to a small mining town, which also had a carbon black factory. Everything there was black, the houses, the dogs, the cows were black, and it was as if even the black hens laid black eggs from which hatched black chicks; a white shirt put on in the morning would be black by evening; and everything smelled of soot. The miners were just as poor and kind and exhausted, the only difference being that they drank not just on Sundays, but after every shift, when they emerged from the mine black with coal dust. But they didn't get drunk so quickly as the fishermen.

It was not by choice but by necessity that Dr Letoni left his home town, where the air was clean and the water pure, and he went first to the fishing village and then to the coal-black town. He left after experiencing the happiest time of his life, which ended in the cruellest disappointment.

Yes, it was a happy time in his life, when he came home from abroad with a fresh piece of parchment inscribed in large black letters, 'Nos Rector…' He was young, he was a doctor, he was in love and was loved, he had a house, a surgery, patients. Yes, he quickly built up a register of patients, starting at the edge of town, visiting the sick on foot, sparing them any great expense, prescribing them inexpensive medicines, curing them not only with medicine but also kind words, encouragement, consolation. And the people began to talk about him, his name began to circulate, and gradually, having started out on the periphery, he began to have patients in the centre of town.

It so happened that some rich merchants – a father and mother – were looking for a university-educated son-in-law for their only daughter, and they found Dr Letoni. Eva, the daughter, was neither ugly, as so often happens in such cases, nor lame, nor humpbacked, but a healthy young woman, a beautiful and intelligent young woman, even. She and Dr Letoni got married according to the wishes of the girl's parents, but also of their own will; they liked each other and fell in love. For a dowry, the girl's parents gave her a house, with a bedroom, dining room, kitchen, outhouses, expensive walnut and ebony furniture, and a surgery complete with instruments and equipment, with a brand-new X-ray machine imported from Germany, and with a metal plate by the door, inscribed with gold letters on a black background: Dr M. Letoni – X-Rays and Diathermy – Consultations, 4 to 8 p.m. But he didn't wait for patients to come to him; he went to them, without taking his carriage, lest he put them to unnecessary expense, and he didn't even look at the fee he was paid. His colleagues spoke ill of him because, so they said, he lowered the dignity of the profession. But he was happy, he loved his work, he loved his patients, he loved his wife, a young, understanding woman, he loved his surgery, where he had everything he needed to cure his patients. And he was able to pay off his debt in instalments.

For Dr Letoni had a large debt to pay. He had borrowed money from his elder brother, who was the accountant at a chemicals and metalwork warehouse and who had supported him throughout his education. His brother was very poor, he had five children and a sick wife, but seeing that his younger brother, the youngest of the family, was good at learning, he thought to lend him the money – such had been their mother's hope and dream, from when the boy was born to the poor woman's death – and after he finished medical school, he would pay him back. The elder brother took the food out of his own children's mouths and sent the youngest brother money for his *mensa*, entering the sum and the date in a ledger. For better or worse, young medical student Martin Letoni was able to eat a modest lunch in the student canteen, and in the morning and the evening, he ate bread and onion, or bread and salt, or nothing at all. The elder brother had added up all the sums in the ledger and Dr Letoni paid them back, in instalments. And he was happy to be able to pay and to work, and the townsfolk used to see him rushing back and forth between patients as if he had wings.

Unfortunately, however, this happiness did not last long. The dark cloud began to gather after his first year of marriage. His wife was still not pregnant and his parents-in-law wanted a grandchild. A year past, a second, a third, and the black cloud grew ever heavier. The young Mrs Letoni took treatments, she was sent to spas, she drank all kinds of mineral waters, she had all kinds of massages, but without result. Her parents, who were practical, calculating folk and, in such matters, very strict, intervened vigorously. What was the point of a marriage without the blessing of children? And they forced their daughter to get a divorce. The girl wept, she and her husband wept night after night, but nothing did it avail them. The girl had been brought up never to go against the word of her mother and father, and in any event, the house and everything in it, down to the last carpet tack, was theirs. Thus it was that after a highly summary court case – for him a surgical operation more painful than the separation of Siamese twins – Dr Letoni found himself banished from paradise, in a condition worse than that of his ancestor Adam, for he found himself out on the street in only the clothes he was wearing, the rest of his wardrobe having remained in the house of his so practical former in-laws, and without his Eve; instead of a vine leaf, he had his doctor's parchment, which, however, could not cover the shame of the all-too-human limits of his medical knowledge.

The so painful separation of the young couple ultimately proved salutary. True, Eva, now a divorcée, didn't find another doctor for a husband. Her parents found her a good match of a different sort, a merchant and manufacturer, a handsome, able young man with a magnificent moustache, who, in a basement on the outskirts of town, ran a so-called 'chemical products factory', where he made boot polish, toothpaste, tea concentrate, parquet creams, and other mixtures, which he himself invented or which the market demanded, and who was constantly in need of injections of capital. All the equipment from the surgery, the shiny silver, nickel and chrome instruments, the X-ray machine, the diathermy apparatus, was sold off as a job lot for less than half it was worth, with the money then immediately flowing into the chemical products factory. In the end, the second husband proved to be a petty charlatan, he went bankrupt, then became a travelling salesman, roaming the length and breadth of the country lugging large suitcases of samples. But be that as it may, this second husband managed to give Eva's parents three grandchildren. As for Dr Letoni, much later he dispelled the ill repute that he had gained at the time by marrying his third wife, the blonde, ambitious Mara, who bore him two children, the children who were to accompany him on his final journey.

But what with one thing and another, after that wretched divorce, Dr Letoni found himself homeless, out on the street, with his doctor's diploma tucked under his arm. His elder brother, the bookkeeper, took him in, let him live in his cramped little house, without adding any further entries to that ledger of his, in his neat, calligraphic hand. What would have been the point, when the youngest brother couldn't even pay off the debts he already had? Before he found that post as a local doctor in that little town black with soot, he lived in his brother's house for months, with his diploma tossed in a drawer; he ate the bread earned through his brother's toil, and continued looking for a job. But in the hospitals, sanatoriums, district surgeries, all the posts were taken.

And how he had toiled and suffered for that doctor's diploma! In foreign cities, always seeking the cheapest lodgings, living in dusty attics or damp cellars, taking meagre meals in the student canteens, eating bread and onion for breakfast and supper, or bread and salt, or nothing at all. And the irony was that his suffering had been prolonged for another year through no fault of his own. Despite being thoroughly prepared, he had been unable to sit his exams due to a ridiculous, tragicomic circumstance.

It was the final examination for his doctorate. His fellow students had all arrived to sit the examination dressed to the nines, some in frock coats, some in smoking jackets. But he had only a single change of clothes, shabby with wear. They entered the examinations room in fives. The professor, a famous cardiologist, was a just man, but strict; he demanded a thorough knowledge of the subject. Martin Letoni felt an attachment to him and knew that the professor valued his hard work. In his turn, the professor felt an attachment to the young student, as he had demonstrated more than once during Martin Letoni's long years of study. But now, during the viva voce, the professor asked the first candidate a question and then the second, before passing on to the fourth and fifth, skipping him, the third, as if he didn't exist. On the next round of questions, he did the same. After the examination was over, the professor said, 'Thank you gentlemen,' and the four left the room. Martin Letoni remained sitting, pale-faced. Rising to his feet, he asked, in a choked voice, 'But you didn't examine me, Professor? Why? Why?'

'Because a doctor's diploma is not awarded to a man so shabbily dressed!' replied the professor, after which he left the room as if personally insulted.

At the next examination, the other students lent him some smart clothes: one gave him a pair of black pinstriped trousers, another a frock coat, another a starched shirt and black necktie. And strangely enough, in those elegant clothes, it was as if he felt more self-assured, as if he had a better command of his subject, and so confident were his answers during the examination that he received his doctorate *summa cum laude*.

He had spent his years at school in a similar fashion, borrowing paper from one, a little ink from another, reading from the other students' textbooks as best he could – he never had books of his own – writing in tiny letters in cheap notebooks without leaving a margin so that it would last as long as possible. He wrote with pencil stumps, pinching them with his fingertips and sharpening them with particular skill and care lest he snap the point. He collected pencil stumps the way other pupils collected cigarette butts to smoke in the toilets on the sly.

He was in the second or third year at primary school when he fell in love with a little girl with dimples in her cheeks and pigtails and a white hairband. His first great love, as secret as it was great. He told nobody in the world, but, God alone knows how, it became known to the rest of the class. He used to talk to her in his mind, he would laugh with her, tell her all kinds of intelligent and amusing things, but when he found himself face to face with her, he couldn't utter a single word. He would remain tongue-tied, blushing. The chubby, sturdy boy with whom he shared a desk – an only child, nicknamed the 'school athlete', always well dressed and cleanly scrubbed – used to give the little girl all kinds of gifts: coloured pencils, steel nibs, erasers. And she accepted them. Why did she accept them? That boy used to laugh and joke with her, as if she were not 'She', but just another girl. Once, he gave her a gilt two-in-one pen and pencil, with a nib at one end and a pencil lead at the other. The girl's eyes glistened in delight. Why had she been so delighted? He, Martin Letoni, who in secret loved her so greatly, was unable to give her anything except his silences. During the breaks, as the children played in the schoolyard, and 'She' talked and frolicked with 'him' – he always thought of 'Her' with a capital letter, whereas the other boy deserved only a small letter. Let always stayed behind in the classroom, for 'Her' sake. 'Let' is what the little girl called him, and how wonderful that syllable sounded when it came from her lips! 'Let, I haven't drawn my map… Let, I didn't have time to write my composition… Let, what did we have for maths homework?' And Let immediately understood, he would blush and stay behind in the classroom during the shorter breaks and at lunchtime, if needed, to do her sums, draw her maps, or write her compositions.

'What do you know?' sounds his voice in my ears, as if from beyond the grave…

Yes, well, this is what we know, what we have been able to discover about Dr Letoni, who has been so much gossiped about and reviled lately, to which the man replied so unexpectedly and simply: by dying suddenly.

And another thing: When he was about to come into the world, the ninth child of a needy family – his father was a poor tailor, a patcher of clothes – he was awaited with mixed feelings. Naturally, his parents, who were simple, pious folk, knew they could not refuse, even in their inmost thoughts, a gift from the Lord Above. But even so, they had eight mouths to feed, ten counting themselves. Eight pairs of shoes, eight sets of clothes for the eldest son and the seven girls who followed him, ten counting their parents. And now the eleventh was about to come into the world.

He was therefore expected as if fated, like a too abundant rain from heaven, which is no longer needed, but which you cannot stop, if the Lord Above so wills it.

But when he was born, the weather-beaten, skilled old midwife suddenly exclaimed: 'The Lord be praised! Born in the water sack… and it's a boy. He was born in his water sack, he'll be a lucky man…'

'He'll be a lucky man,' repeated his mother, drained of strength.

'He'll be a lucky man,' repeated his father, caressing the poor woman's sweating brow.

'Our little brother will be a lucky man,' repeated the eight children, waiting in the kitchen.

'Who knows, maybe he'll even become a doctor,' said his mother, falling into a peaceful, restful sleep.

# The Author

The writer LUDOVIC ( Joseph-Leib, Arye) BRUCKSTEIN was born on the 27th of July 1920, in Munkacs, then in Czechoslovakia, now in Ukraine. He grew up in Sighet, a small town in the district of Maramureş, in the Northern region of Transylvania, a town well known for its flourishing pre-war Jewish community and Hassidic tradition. He wrote a number of successful plays including *The Night Shift* (*Nacht-Shicht*, 1947), based on the Sonder-kommando revolt in Auschwitz. His other works include *The Confession* (a novel, 1973), *The Destiny of Yaakov Maggid* (seven short stories, 1975), *Three Histories* (three short historical stories, 1977), *The Tinfoil Halo* (short stories, 1979), *As in Heaven, so on Earth* (short stories, 1981), *Maybe Even Happiness* (short stories, 1985), *The Murmur of Water* (short stories, 1987).
 *The Trap* (two novellas) appeared posthumously in 1989.

# The Translator

ALISTAIR IAN BLYTH is one of the most active translators working from Romanian into English today. A native of Sunderland, England, Blyth has resided for many years in Bucharest. His many translations from Romanian include: *Little Fingers* by Filip Florian; *Our Circus Presents* by Lucian Dan Teodorovici; *Coming from an Off-Key Time* by Bogdan Suceavă; and *Life Begins on Friday* by Ioana Pârvulescu.

*I don't know whether or not God exists, I know only that God was with him. When the time comes – time sometimes lifts the whiteness from the eyes of the descendants, when the time comes, as I say, to draw up not the literary statistics of a period, but the just history of writing in Romanian from all over the world, it will be discovered that here among us in the last two decades there lived an authentic writer. In the non-pecuniary market of mental stocks, Ludovic Bruckstein was not a needy petitioner, but an aristocrat of the word, of ideas, of analytical strength, of expression. A great writer. A romantic philosopher, who knew how to drive a cart up a hill in the Maramureș sleet. He knew how a man is built up and knocked down how daily bread is earned. Above all, he knew how a life is wasted. Reread him, esteemed reader. He loved you, he always sought the way to your heart.*

Iosif Petran

*Revista mea*, 12 August 1988

*Some twenty-five years ago, when I was still a child, the Jewish Theatre troupe arrived from Bucharest in my provincial town (Bîrlad), bringing Ludovic Bruckstein's play Nightshift. It was set in Auschwitz, the drama was powerful, the audience wept, and I was left with the conviction that such a play could only be written by a writer who died along with his characters.*
*Years later, when I met him at the Literature School in Bucharest, I was very disappointed that he was still alive. To reassure me, he confessed that he had indeed died in Auschwitz, and also when he wrote the play, and above all when the censors forced him to make changes to it. But he was constantly forced to return to life, since he had a host of obligations as a husband, a father, and a writer.*

I. Schechter

*Izvoare*, No. 5, Tel Aviv, 1978

First published in 2020 by
**Istros Books**
London, United Kingdom www.istrosbooks.com

Copyright © Estate of Ludovic Bruckstein, 2020

This collection of stories first appeared in Hebrew translation as
*Mitriya Sgura BeGeshem Oferet* at Nimrod, Tel Aviv, in 2006

The right of Ludovic Bruckstein, to be identified as the author of this work has been
asserted in accordance with the Copyright, Designs and Patents Act, 1988

Translation © Alistair Ian Blyth

Typesetting: Davor Pukljak, www.frontispis.hr
Illustrations: Alfred M. Bruckstein
Cover picture of L. Bruckstein taken by Rita Bruckstein, 1987

ISBN: 978-1-912545-22-3

The publishers would like to express their thanks for the financial
support that made the publication of this book possible:
The Prodan Romanian Cultural Foundation and the Arts Council England

PRODAN ROMANIAN
CULTURAL FOUNDATION

9 781912 545223